PRAISE FOR ARIEL S. WINTER
AND *BARREN COVE*

"A meticulously imagined story that reads like *The Wasp Factory* soldered into *Do Androids Dream of Electric Sheep?* The pages really skittered by. Genuinely literary science fiction."

—Natasha Pulley, author of the internationally bestselling
The Watchmaker of Filigree Street

"Providing further evidence of the futility of genre labels, *Barren Cove* is a thoughtful and affecting family drama that just happens to be about robots. Winter's vision of a machine-ruled dystopia is a quiet country manor where a few mechanical people search for meaning in the mysteries of their programming. An unsettling portrait of humanity as seen through the eyes of its creations."

—Isaac Marion, *New York Times* bestselling author of
Warm Bodies and *The Burning World*

"*Barren Cove* is a touching and funny and skillfully written novel, and an original take on science fiction. I'm not a great fan of this genre, but I can see, with this one book, how Mr. Winter could make me one. The writing is clean and highly readable; the characters are believable, despite being robots; the dialog is ear-perfect, and the plot never sags or lets up for a minute. I had a great time reading it."

—Stephen Dixon, National Book Award–nominated
author of *Frog* and *Interstate*

"Weaves a uniquely dreamy spell, and a lingering one. Lyrical, unexpected, and curiously affecting . . . [A] story that lodges uneasily in the heart and mind."

—*Kirkus Reviews*

"A quietly brilliant look at what it means to be human. This deserves to be a classic."

—*Booklist* (starred review)

"From the first line to the last, I loved every page, my brain lighting up in strange and wonderful ways."

—*The Literate Quilter*

"Ariel S. Winter has created a masterful work in *Barren Cove*. His writing style flows beautifully and ensnared me before I quite comprehended where he was taking me."

—*Popcorn Reads*

"Winter's plot-line is drenched in risk, but he's able to pull it off via layered characters who speak in universal tones about the world which we share."

—*Electric Review*

PRAISE FOR ARIEL S. WINTER'S
THE TWENTY-YEAR DEATH

"Bold, innovative and thrilling."

—Stephen King, *New York Times* bestselling author

"Extraordinary . . . seductive, even a little sinister . . . like some glittering spider web that catches the eye of an admiring fly."

—Marilyn Stasio, *The New York Times*

"An absolute astonishment."

—Peter Straub, *New York Times* bestselling author of *A Dark Matter*

"Wildly, audaciously original."

—James Frey, *New York Times* bestselling author of *A Million Little Pieces*

"[A] delight."

—Alice Sebold, *New York Times* bestselling author of *The Lovely Bones*

"A testament to style . . . [a] triumph."

—*Los Angeles Times*

"Marvelous."

—*The Washington Post*

"Tight, compact, and riveting."

—*City Paper* (Baltimore)

"Winter carries his tri-fold tale off with consummate skill. . . . [A] groundbreaking crime epic."

—*SeattlePI.com*

"Sometimes a first novel appears that is so bold, so innovative, so brilliant that you just have to tip your hat and say 'Bravo.' . . . [It's] as if Winter decided to show up at Yankee Stadium determined to hit with Babe Ruth's bat and belted a home run first time at the plate. . . . Transcendent."

—*Bookreporter*

"Audacious and astonishingly executed . . . immersive, exhilarating, and revelatory."

—*Booklist* (starred review)

"A hell of a lot of fun."

—*Publishers Weekly*

"Brilliant."

—*Library Journal* (starred review)

ALSO BY ARIEL S. WINTER

Barren Cove

The Twenty-Year Death

THE
PRESERVE

a novel

ARIEL S. WINTER

EMILY BESTLER BOOKS
—
ATRIA
NEW YORK LONDON TORONTO SYDNEY NEW DELHI

EMILY
BESTLER
BOOKS

ATRIA

An Imprint of Simon & Schuster, Inc.
1230 Avenue of the Americas
New York, NY 10020

This book is a work of fiction. Any references to historical events, real people, or real places are used fictitiously. Other names, characters, places, and events are products of the author's imagination, and any resemblance to actual events or places or persons, living or dead, is entirely coincidental.

First Emily Bestler Books/Atria Paperback edition November 2020

EMILY BESTLER BOOKS/ATRIA PAPERBACK and colophon are trademarks of Simon & Schuster, Inc.

For information about special discounts for bulk purchases, please contact Simon & Schuster Special Sales at 1-866-506-1949 or business@simonandschuster.com.

The Simon & Schuster Speakers Bureau can bring authors to your live event. For more information, or to book an event, contact the Simon & Schuster Speakers Bureau at 1-866-248-3049 or visit our website at http://www.simonspeakers.com.

Interior design by Kyoko Watanabe
Publisher: Emily Bestler
Editor: Lara Jones
Agent: Edward Maxwell
Managing editors: Paige Lytle, Jessie McNiel
Production editor: Mark LaFlaur
Copyeditor: Tricia Callahan
Publicist: Mirtha Pena
Marketing: Maudee Genao
Art director: James Iacobelli
Production manager: Vanessa Silverio
Desktop: Hope Herr-Cardillo

Manufactured in the United States of America

1 3 5 7 9 10 8 6 4 2

Library of Congress Cataloging-in-Publication Data has been applied for.

ISBN 978-1-4767-9788-5
ISBN 978-1-4767-9790-8 (ebook)

THE
PRESERVE

Sitting down, chief of police Jesse Laughton put his palms on his desk to steady himself, closed his eyes, and took a deep breath. He was exhausted. His headache, coupled with the chronic pain in his face, made it hard to focus. *Life would be easier if I was dead*, he thought, then opened his eyes and looked at the clock on the wall without turning his head. The thin red hand made its stuttering march through the numbers into the late afternoon. Only forty-three minutes left in his shift.

Then the phone on his desk buzzed, the vibration sliding it across the out-of-date calendar-blotter. He had it set on Do Not Disturb, and lying facedown. He knew that having his phone in Do Not Disturb mode during his shift was not only against the police department's bylaws, but as chief was irresponsible. But this late in the day, he just didn't care. Now it was ringing anyway, which meant that somebody needed to get through badly enough to call him more than once in two minutes. Still, he watched it buzz for another few seconds before working up the strength to turn it over to see who was calling. It was Mathews. That was bad.

He answered. "Chief Laughton."

"Well, we won the lottery," Mathews said without a hello.

Laughton felt his stomach drop, followed by a wave of nausea. He waited for it.

"Dead body," Mathews said. "Taser to the neck."

Laughton closed his eyes again. "Homicide."

"Looks like it. First one on the preserve."

Shit. Nine months since they opened the SoCar Preserve, and the first body has to show up in Liberty. Really, it's amazing it took this long. The drop in violent crime since the preserve opened was something both the robot and preserve governments were touting as proof that the preserve had been a success that far exceeded expectations. Well, the honeymoon was over.

"It's Carl Smythe. Body was behind Kramer's Market, between the dumpster and the loading dock. I thought you'd want to come look."

Chief Laughton could feel his left lower eyelid fluttering. The whole left side of his face began to tingle.

"Chief?"

"Anything I can't get from the pictures?" he said.

"It's just when they start asking questions," Mathews said, "they're going to be asking you."

Why did it have to be in Liberty?

"Okay," Laughton said. "I'll be right over."

"We'll be waiting."

Chief Laughton hung up, and held the phone a moment in a daze. He looked at the clock again. It promised thirty-seven minutes left in his shift, but that didn't mean anything now. If only his head didn't hurt. He opened his desk drawer and took out a bottle of Advil. Each pill cost a fortune these days, but if there was ever a time to use them, this was it, even if he knew they probably wouldn't help. He swallowed four, dry, dropped the bottle back in the desk drawer, and looked at his gun sitting in the drawer as well. The way his face felt, he couldn't shoot straight if he had to. There was no reason to make the first murder in preserve history also the first day he carried a gun since coming to Liberty. He slammed the drawer shut, stood, and strode out of the room.

———

Liberty was the smallest of the three towns on the preserve outside of Charleston. The town had started out with a larger than normal human population because of two separate Southern Baptist churches that had attracted strong congregations. That gave it a reputation of being orgo-friendly, and the churches had advertised that all were welcome. Now that Liberty was overflowing with preservationists, the churches' importance had waned. The town instead sported more bars than any other kind of establishment, and they were all lax with whom they served and how much.

Chief Laughton pulled his truck up to where Mathews's cruiser was parked. The blacktop was cracked, green shoots growing where they could. A chunk of concrete sat beside the supermarket's loading dock, a rusty bit of rebar at the edge of the platform showing where it had been. There were two dumpsters, both overflowing, and garbage bags neatly lined up on the ground all around them. A refrigerated box truck, its compressor huddled on top, was backed up against the loading bay with a crude painting of a cornucopia emblazoned on the side. The word "Sisters" was written in fancy script above the cornucopia, and stenciled block letters below it read "SoCar Preserve."

Mathews and his partner, Dunrich, were talking to Larry Richman, the store's manager, and some skinny, white kid, looked maybe fifteen. The kid had his arms folded high on his chest, hands in his armpits, like he was cold despite the early spring weather. A young black man sucking a vape leaned against the delivery truck. Richman kept peeking over his shoulder at the body slumped against the building. *Jesus*, Laughton thought. He put the truck in reverse, and pulled it back so that it blocked the view of the body for anyone who happened to be going by. They didn't need an audience.

The chief willed his mind to focus, pushing the pain in his face and his head down as best he could to get through the job that needed to be done. He got out of his truck, and Mathews turned to meet his boss.

"The kid found him when he came out to receive the delivery," Mathews said without bothering with a greeting.

Carl Smythe's body was propped up in the corner formed by the loading dock and the back of the building. He was wearing cargo shorts and a three-quarter-sleeve baseball shirt for some team called the Cougars. His head was tilted back, his eyes closed. "You close the eyes?" Laughton said.

Mathews shook his head. "They were like that."

Laughton nodded. The eyes hardly mattered. The real showstopper was Smythe's left arm and leg. They'd both been cut open, jagged tears consistent with a dull blade. But instead of a bloody mass of flesh, the wounds revealed metal bones encased in simul-skin. "So he was a robot," Laughton said. "Shit."

"Cyborg," Mathews said.

"You knew?"

"Nah. We did a scan when we saw the bones. Rest of him's one hundred percent orgo."

"Hate crime?"

Mathews shook his head and shrugged. "I don't see it. Records search said Smythe was into sims."

Laughton pulled out his phone and took a picture of the corpse.

"We got it on the 3-D," Mathews said.

"A picture comes in handy," Laughton said, checking it. "Black guy the deliveryman?"

"Yeah." Mathews looked at his phone. "Barry Slattery. He doesn't have a record."

Laughton examined the area around the body, but there was nothing to find. It wasn't like there would be footprints in the asphalt. "You said it was a Taser?"

"I didn't want to move him, but you can just see it, back of the neck."

Laughton stepped closer to the body. He saw the discoloration Mathews was talking about. "Give me gloves."

Mathews pulled a pair of black latex gloves from his pocket and handed them to the chief.

After putting them on, Laughton tilted the head forward with great care, as though he didn't want to wake the man, and there, in the center of the back of the neck, were twin puncture wounds, swollen like bee stings, reminiscent of vampire bites from old horror movies. "Good spot, Officer."

"Could be a robot," Mathews said.

"Or it could just be a Taser."

"Weird choice of murder weapon."

"Unless Smythe wasn't supposed to die."

Laughton ran his hands down to the pockets. "Phone?"

Mathews shook his head. "Couldn't find it."

"Boss?" Dunrich called.

Laughton and Mathews turned.

"You want to talk to these guys?"

"Did he really just do that?" Laughton said to Mathews. He shook his head and rolled his eyes, and headed for the witnesses.

Larry Richman was in his familiar suit, the jacket over a black T-shirt with no tie. Laughton wondered if Bob Kramer required the outfit of his manager, or if Larry wore it out of pride. He had been the sole supplier of food to the human population back when Liberty was still named after some extinct Native American tribe, before its new residents rechristened it as an outgrowth of the upwelling optimism many felt at the creation of the preserve. The demotion from owner to manager had to sting, even if it had been Larry's decision to sell his store to Kramer. It always struck Laughton as a bit ridiculous to see Larry restocking shelves or carrying boxes all dressed up.

"Hey, Larry," Laughton said.

"Jesse," Larry said.

The boy wore a Kramer's collared T-shirt and black pants. His name tag read "Ryan." In Baltimore, Chief Laughton had been the only human in major crimes, famous for reading lies on people's faces that robotic facial recognition software could never match, but on the preserve, there hadn't been much cause to call on his nearly fifteen years of experience. That'd been the point of the job, after all. It was supposed to be stress-free, or at least stress-lite, given the smaller population, but as he began talking to the boy, he immediately started to evaluate the muscle movement in the boy's face, reading his macro-expressions while looking for any micro-expressions that might flitter by.

"Ryan," Laughton said, turning to the boy, "you already tell the officers what you saw?"

"We've got it recorded, boss," Dunrich said.

Laughton didn't even bother to turn to give his officer the evil eye for interrupting. He could count on Mathews to reprimand his partner later. "Tell me," Laughton said.

"There's not much to tell, really. I came out of the back"—he nodded, indicating which door with his chin—"Barry was opening the back of the truck, and I looked over and just . . ."

nose wrinkle, cheeks raised, eyebrows down—disgust

"I saw the body."

"And?"

"I told Mr. Richman," Ryan said.

face neutral

"I thought I was going to throw up."

Laughton felt that way too, but it had nothing to do with the crime scene. Trying to ignore his headache was getting harder. "Did you know who it was?"

The boy shook his head.

nose wrinkle softened, cheeks relax—relief

"Never seen him."

"See any strangers around? Unfamiliar cars?"

The boy shook his head again. *Consistent expression.*

Laughton looked at Larry. *Eyelids raised, rest of face passive—worry.* Laughton couldn't say whether it was for the victim, who was beyond help, or for how the event would affect his business. "Larry?"

"I've seen him around," the manager said.

lower eyelids tensing—fear

"Came in maybe once a week or so, maybe. I didn't know his name."

"What about Barry?" Laughton said, lowering his voice. "How well you know him?"

lower eyelids relaxed—fear passed as he realized he wouldn't be asked anything he didn't know

"He's been making the produce delivery for a while, before the preserve, maybe two years? I don't know."

"You ever seen him talking to the victim?"

frown, grooves flanking the lips, narrowed lower eyelids—answer in the negative

"Nah," Larry said. "Barry doesn't come in past the storeroom. He drops the stuff and pulls out."

Laughton looked over at the deliveryman. His right leg was jiggling with nerves as he took another drag from his vape.

"Cameras back here?"

"No. No reason to waste the electricity."

"What about inside? Or in the front?"

Larry shook his head. "Theft hasn't been a problem. Mr. Kramer figures anyone stealing probably needs it anyway."

"Haven't I seen those tinted domes in the ceiling?"

"Just for show." Even the worry was gone now, and no micro-expressions to counter anything the manager had said. Neither of them was lying, which wasn't really a surprise.

Laughton looked at the body again. Why'd it have to be in his jurisdiction? Gangs had sprung up in the city. Couldn't *they* shoot each other? "We'll have to ask the other employees if they noticed anyone."

"Of course," Larry said.

The chief knew he should have other questions, but he couldn't think straight, the tension in his face making everything fuzzy. "Okay," Laughton said, feeling unsettled. "Let me know if you think of anything or see anything."

"What about the body?" Larry said.

"We'll have it out of here soon."

That seemed to satisfy the store manager. What else was he going to do?

"Listen," Laughton said. "Don't tell anybody about this, and if you told anyone already, tell them not to tell anyone. I want to keep this close as long as we can." Laughton looked everyone in the eye, and they all nodded. "All right," he said. He held out his hand. "Thanks, Larry."

They shook. Then Richman led the stock boy to the rusted, handleless back door, took a ring of keys from his pocket, sorted through them, and opened the door.

Laughton turned his attention to the deliveryman. He was still bouncing his leg.

"What *do* we do with the body?" Mathews said.

In Baltimore, they would have a forensics team in to record the crime scene in hyper-definition, but they didn't have those kinds of resources in Liberty. They also didn't have a place to store a corpse. He guessed he'd have to at least loop in the coroner—if there even was a coroner—which meant they wouldn't be able to keep this to themselves for long. "Call for the ambulance," he said. "It's not like we have any fancy CSI we can do here, and the city can't get anyone out here in something like a reasonable time. I'm going to talk to the deliveryman."

"Dunrich," Mathews called. The younger officer was squatting near the body, examining who knows what. "Radio for the ambulance."

Dunrich put his hands on his thighs and pushed himself up. He tore his eyes away with reluctance, going over to the cruiser and reaching in for the radio.

As Laughton approached the deliveryman, the young man's shoulders went up, and he turned just a few degrees, a defensive pose.

"Evening," Laughton said. "Barry?"

The young man sucked on his vape and nodded.

"You want to tell me what happened?"

Despite the body language, the man's face was relatively neutral. "Not much to tell, boss. I didn't see the guy until the kid said, 'Shit. Oh my god.' "

flash of nose wrinkle, slight upper lip raise—disgust at the memory

"How didn't you see the guy before then? Body's pretty obvious."

Barry shook his head. "Look, I got out of the cab and walked around the front of the truck, so the truck was blocking my view. I wasn't looking all around or anything."

"What about in the side mirror when you were backing up the truck."

"Man, then I'm looking at the edge of the truck and the loading dock. I'm not taking in the whole scene."

People can often miss things that are right in front of them. Their minds are somewhere else, and they're moving without even seeing their surroundings. You could walk right past your brother in a crowd and never even see him. Still, Laughton didn't love it. The body was pretty obvious.

"Do you know the guy?" Laughton said. "Look familiar?" *micro-expression—sadness—lying?*

"I don't think so."

"You don't think so, or you know?"

"No," Barry said, shaking his head. "I don't know him."

Laughton waited a beat, giving Barry a chance to add something, to change his answer. But instead, the deliveryman covered his expression by taking another drag of his vape.

"Where do you live?" Laughton said.

"Charleston."

"And you deliver anywhere else?"

"The whole preserve. Beaufort, Georgetown. This is my last stop."

"Can I see inside the truck?"

Barry nodded. "Sure." He led Laughton around the front of the truck, up the stairs to the loading dock, and pulled the back of the truck open. It was empty, and cold from the refrigeration unit. Laughton's footsteps echoed as he walked in. There were a few leaves of lettuce crushed into the floor of the truck. A hand truck was bungeed to the wood slats along the inside left wall. Laughton stepped back onto the loading dock, and he noticed that the body wasn't visible from there. Barry wouldn't have seen it while unloading the truck.

"You're heading back to Charleston now?"

Barry nodded. "Yeah."

That micro-expression bothered the chief. People generally didn't show sadness over the death of a stranger, but it could have just as easily been sadness that he couldn't help. But if he had been involved in the murder, Laughton would have expected fear or anger. "All right," Laughton said. "We might need to contact you again. Can we get your info?"

Barry took his phone out of his back pocket, and Laughton tapped his phone against it. There was the confirming buzz of receipt. Then Barry grabbed the canvas strap hanging from the truck's back door and pulled the door shut with a clang.

Laughton hopped down from the loading dock, joining Mathews as Barry locked up the back of the truck.

"Carl was living over in Crofton," Mathews said. "Whole town to himself, except Sam something-or-other. I think they were living together."

"Shit," Laughton said. He closed his eyes and sighed. "We better go talk to him in case he decides it's time for a road trip." He opened his eyes and tried to calculate if he needed to let his counterparts in the other inhabited towns of the preserve know the situation. There was nothing the chiefs of police in Beaufort and Georgetown could do. Chris Ontero, the police commissioner in Charleston, was technically not his superior, but as the head of the police in the preserve's one large city, the commissioner was the face of preserve law enforcement. He would have to talk to the press when this went wide.

"You sure you're okay, Chief?"

"No," Laughton said. "Just give me a moment." He pulled his phone out of his pocket and called the Charleston Police Department. As it rang he said to Mathews, "Come on. You've got driver's seat." He headed for his truck while Mathews told his partner to wait for the ambulance. The delivery truck pulled away from the building, Barry leaning back in his seat in the cab.

The CPD system shuffled the chief around until he got a voice mail recording. He didn't want to leave the news on the phone—he didn't know if a secretary answered the commissioner's voice mail—so he just left a message asking the commissioner to call him. He stepped up into the passenger seat, texting his wife with one hand, the auto-suggest anticipating each word, allowing him to just tap: "I'll be home late." Either it was something he texted often enough for the phone's memory to fill in the blanks or it was such a common thing to say—thousands of people always late, always apologizing— that it was in the phone's programming. He dropped his phone in the cup holder, and let his head fall back on the headrest and closed his eyes. If only the pain would stop.

Mathews jumped into the driver's seat, pushing the power button before he'd even gotten the door closed. "Battery's a little low, boss."

"It'll be fine," Laughton said without opening his eyes. His phone buzzed twice. It was probably his wife responding to his text. He didn't bother to get the phone out to check.

Then something in his head clicked on. *Timing*, he thought. He put down the window, and called, "Dunrich."

Dunrich looked up from his phone, and then jogged over to the truck. "Boss?" he said.

"Find out how often they take the garbage out," the chief said. "Give us some idea of how long the body might have been sitting here."

"Okay."

"And ask the other employees about strangers."

"Right."

Laughton raised the window. He should have thought of the timing question when he was interviewing Larry and Ryan. This didn't bode well, if his mind was this fuzzy. What else had he forgotten to ask?

"Ready?" Mathews said.

The chief nodded.

Mathews punched "Crofton" into the GPS, and the truck managed a U-turn, the whole cab bouncing as they went through a pothole. The junior officer, mercifully, didn't say anything.

I t was just falling dusk as they made their way through Crofton. The front lawns of all the houses had gone to hay, about knee-high, and there wasn't a single electric light on anywhere. Even the streetlights were dark. The robots must have figured, *Why waste the bulbs?*, and took them with them. Otherwise, it was hard to know the town was deserted. The houses had been inhabited recently enough that they'd yet to show signs of ruin. A United States flag hung from a flagpole in front of one home. Solar panels remained on many roofs, harder to take away than lightbulbs. Porch furniture waited loyally for sitters that would never come. Laughton could never decide if the robots had afforded humans so much land to humor the pro-orgos, who thought consolidating humans would encourage a population boom that'd require space to grow into, or if the machines just wanted a wide cushion zone.

The two policemen didn't know where Smythe had been living, so they meandered up and down the backstreets, Mathews driving manually. He turned on the headlights, then about twenty minutes later, the brights. The lights turned the hay a yellow white, and the black shadows of the houses rising from the wild lawns made Laughton think of old pictures he'd seen of elephants on the savannah, although he didn't know how big elephants had really been and couldn't imagine an animal that large.

The chief's headache had receded just enough to be nagging instead of debilitating. He kept rubbing his face to stay awake.

When he saw the glow of artificial lights one street over, he exhaled in relief. "There," he said.

Mathews looked, and then gunned the engine, pulling around the corner on screeching tires.

"Jesus, Mathews," Laughton said.

"Sorry."

The house was a plain, bloated, two-story box, probably a hundred years old, from a time when size was more important than style. The light escaping from the open windows showed rows of solar panels covering the front lawn and the lawns of both neighbors. Thick wires hung from the roof where there must have been another array. The solar panels explained how Smythe and Sam could afford the extravagant show of light, but that many solar panels weren't just being used for night-time illumination. Something was happening in the house.

"Looks like Sam hasn't gone anywhere," Mathews said.

"Looks it."

"How do you want to do this?"

The chief opened his door. "We're just going to have a conversation," he said, stepping down from the truck. Mathews got out on the other side, and they slammed the doors. No need to worry about alerting the man. They were about to knock.

As the men made their way down the narrow path, a backlit silhouette appeared in one of the front windows, peering out to see who had arrived. It moved quickly away from the window at the sight of them. They opened the storm door, and Laughton banged on the front door with the side of his closed fist. Mathews turned on his body camera. The chief still liked to take notes with a stylus and oversize phone. "Look," Mathews said, a smile in his voice. Laughton looked and saw the calm, slow pulses of fireflies hovering among the solar panels.

The door swung open. The chief squinted against the sudden brightness, which stabbed him in the right eye. A rail-thin man in his early thirties stood looking at them. He wore glasses with no bottom rims, and had his hair in a ponytail, stray wisps floating around his head. A tattoo graced the inside of his forearm, something in fancy calligraphy that the chief couldn't read.

"Yes?" the man said, his tone an attempt at being calm but ruined by a note of defensiveness.

Mathews *was* in uniform. Laughton took his badge folder from his rear pocket, and flipped it open for the man to see. "This is Officer Mathews. I'm Chief Laughton. May we come in?"

The man hesitated, seeming on the verge of asking a question, but then stepped back and said, "Sure, okay."

The policemen stepped by him into a small but cavernous entryway, the ceiling extending up to the second story. A carpeted room to the left was filled with industrial metal shelving laden with row after row of chunky, gamer-level computer towers, each with a small green LED eye assuring it was on. It was hot inside, despite the open windows. The combined noise of the computers' cooling fans sounded like rushing water.

"That's a lot of hardware," Mathews said, turning his body so the camera was sure to pick it up.

"Yeah," the man said with a nervous, embarrassed laugh.

"What's your name, sir?" Chief Laughton said, getting out his phone and opening a new note.

"Sam McCardy," he said. "Samuel."

"And you live here with Carl Smythe."

"We're business partners."

"What's your business?" Mathews said.

McCardy looked like he could punch himself. "Computers," he said.

Mathews snuffed in amusement.

"When was the last time you saw Mr. Smythe?" Laughton asked.

"I don't know," McCardy said. "Lunchtime? Right before lunch."

"What time was that?"

The man's brow screwed up in serious contemplation. He shook his head. "Eleven." He shrugged. "I really don't know. Did something happen with Carl?"

"As a matter of fact," Laughton said, "he's dead."

McCardy went white, his whole body slumping, his breathing grew shallow, and his mouth screwed up, the look of a man who was refusing to allow himself to cry. He tested out his voice, and it came out cracked. "How?" Just the one word.

screwed-up lips, lower eyelids narrowed—grief

"Mr. McCardy. Could we come in, maybe sit down?" Chief Laughton said. The grief seemed genuine, but there was a flash of fear in the brow. Not uncommon given the situation, but suppressed faster than Laughton would have expected.

"Yeah," McCardy said, nodding, looking at the ground, looking at nothing. "Sure. Yeah." He stepped back, and then turned, leading them through a small passage into a combined kitchen–living room space. Here there was more industrial shelving surrounding two large folding tables in the center of the room, each with three flat-panel monitors, multiple VR headsets, keyboards, enormous speakers on stands, and what looked like large soundboards with rows of tiny dials. The shelving was not given over entirely to computers, though. There was a retro-gaming rig with some antique consoles going back to the twentieth century. Chief Laughton recognized a few consoles from his father's collection with a pang of nostalgia. Confusingly, there were two racks stuffed with books—real, antique, paper books—more than Laughton had ever seen outside of a museum. More than he'd ever seen *inside* a museum.

But of course, the thing that drew his eye was bins filled with different-colored memory sticks, the kind that was used for sims. Each bin was marked with masking tape on which code names were written: *Dikdik, Mollies, Starburst, The Bat.* Chief Laughton still did not understand why sims remained a physical medium. The programming—human or robot—the manufacture of memory sticks, the distribution, the porting, the whole physical supply chain necessary for human drugs seemed like a reckless danger for something that could be handled in code remotely. He understood that sims were written in such a way that they deleted both from the memory stick and from the robot's short-term memory as the program ran so that no copy of the program was retained, making it onetime use. That, of course, was necessary if it was going to be a salable commodity, but also, it seemed, was preferable to robots, because it meant that the experience could not be repeated, especially since a well-written sim filled in elements taken from the external environment and the robot's memory, making each experience of the sim unique. But none of those things seemed to make physical memory sticks essential, based on his human understanding of the experience.

Sometimes Laughton wondered if the whole illegal-sims operation took the shape it did to purposely ape historical human drug trafficking, if the construct of the illegal behaviors around the act of sims use was an intrinsic part of a robot's enjoyment of the experience.

They all looked at the setup for a moment in silence, as though even McCardy needed to take it in.

Laughton stepped into the room, and Mathews said to McCardy, "You want to sit down?"

McCardy nodded, and in a daze went to one of the desk chairs in the center of the room. "What the hell happened?" he said.

"We're trying to figure that out," Mathews said.

"I mean, what the hell happened?" McCardy said again.

"What do you mean?" Mathews said.

Chief Laughton watched McCardy's face, and said, "He was murdered."

eyes closed, lips tightened—pain

"No," McCardy said, shaking his head. "No, no, no, no."

"Is there someone who would have wanted to hurt him?" Mathews said.

"No. Wait. Of course. Look at this shit." He looked back and forth at the policemen. "It's all legal," he hurried to say, not fooling anyone, "of course, all legal. But you know. Sims . . ."

Laughton walked over to the rack of books and pulled one off the shelf at random. *Blended Worlds.* He pulled a few more out. *The Hidden Triangle. The Twenty-Year Death.* He'd never heard of any of them. The things seemed one step away from dust.

"Did you know that Mr. Smythe was a cyborg?" Mathews said.

"Yeah. Of course. What does that matter? You think it was because he was a cyborg?"

"It's possible. Are you a cyborg?"

McCardy jerked back like he'd tasted something unexpectedly bad. "What? No. Not that there's anything wrong with that. They're humans first. They have the same rights to be on the preserve, and everything."

"No one's saying anything against cyborgs," Chief Laughton said, putting the books back on the shelf. "Where'd you get all of these books?"

"What does it fucking matter?" The shock over his friend's death had turned to anger, eyebrows lowered, pulled together.

"I've just never seen so many books. Why do you have them?"

"Metals like human-written sims because of the messed-up shit we can think up that they can't. Old books give us a lot of stuff to use. Those are all crap books that no one thought were worth digitizing, so metals have never seen them."

"Who's your distributor?" Mathews said.

McCardy turned back to the officer, caught off balance between the two men. He hesitated.

"Look, we don't care about your sims," Laughton said. "We're not here to bust anyone on sims. That's a metals problem, not a preserve problem as far as I'm concerned. But we need to find who killed your friend. And we need the names of anyone who might be able to help."

McCardy's shoulders slumped. "Something Jones. Carl handled all of that, and he just always said Jones. Crap, what am I going to do now?"

Laughton met Mathews's eyes. The officer gave a slight shake of the head; he didn't know the name Jones either.

"Was he in town to meet Jones?"

"No, he'd just gone for groceries."

"And you stayed here?"

"Yes."

"You were here all day? Didn't go to town too?"

"I haven't left the house." He said it matter-of-factly, without the insistence of someone trying to establish an alibi. He didn't even seem to consider that was what was being asked.

"Did Carl have family?" Laughton said.

"Just a sister. His dad died when he was little. His mom was killed in a car crash. That's how he lost his arm and leg. He isn't some modder," he said, defending his friend. "He actually needs those prosthetics."

"Does his sister live on the preserve?"

McCardy shook his head. "Oakland. She was paralyzed in the crash. She's more machine than orgo. Says she's happier out there."

If she'd been paralyzed, there was no way she could blend. Despite McCardy's egalitarianism, a cyborg that couldn't blend wouldn't be particularly popular on the preserve.

"Friends? Anyone else we should talk to?"

"I don't know," McCardy said. "Some robots, before we moved to the preserve. He did all of the runs into town. Maybe he knew some people there."

"Yeah. Okay," Laughton said. "What's his sister's name?"

"Cindy."

"Do you have her contact info? We couldn't find Smythe's phone."

McCardy fumbled for the phone on his desk, swiped through, and then looking up at the chief, extended his phone.

Laughton caught Mathews's eye and gave a slight nod. The junior officer took his own phone and tapped it to McCardy's.

"I'm giving you my info too," Mathews said, "if you think of anything else once we leave . . ."

McCardy nodded.

"He didn't leave his phone here, by any chance, did he?"

McCardy frowned, and shook his head. "No."

"We'll need to go through Mr. Smythe's computer," Chief Laughton said.

"I don't know the password."

"We'll get experts out here tomorrow to go through it all."

"Tomorrow," McCardy repeated, not a question, just a sound.

"You sure there's no way you could get in, maybe help us out."

"Carl perfected the burner, a program that literally sets a computer on fire. If he didn't want anyone on his machine, there's no way on."

"Our man will give it a try," Laughton said, but he didn't have much faith that it would yield anything. If the hard drive didn't get burned out, these guys were too cagey to leave a trail of any kind. "And what was Jones's first name again?" the chief said, circling back on the question in the hopes of shaking loose an answer.

"I don't know," McCardy said with the first twinge of annoyance.

"I find that a little hard to believe," the chief said.

"Why? I didn't deal with him. Carl never said."

"You're a sims hacker, but you have no idea how your product is sold, where the money comes from? Come on, Sam. You know that sounds ridiculous."

"I'm a hacker. That's *all* I know. Look around. I don't even leave the house. And the one person I do see, you're telling me is dead." His face crumpled, and tears slid down each cheek, but he managed to avoid a full breakdown.

"We just want to find the person that killed your partner," the chief said. "Given the business you're in, it seems most likely to be related. Any names you could give us . . ."

McCardy opened his mouth, but closed it again, pressing his lips together in order to avoid losing control of his feelings. When the danger of crying had passed, he opened his mouth again, but the first words came out as a choke, and he had to swallow and repeat himself. "I really have nothing to do with the business side. Carl does all of that. This guy Jones moves it to a larger distributor who gets it off the preserve, I don't know who. And then, I guess, I don't know, metals?"

He really didn't know. There were plenty of husbands who didn't know what bills got paid because their wives took care of them. It must have been like that. "Okay," Laughton said. There were only so many times the man could swallow his tears. If they pushed him too far, he'd be reluctant to come to them with more information later. "If you hear from Jones, though," Laughton said, "let us know."

McCardy had receded into his shell again. "Yeah. Of course."

"I'm sorry about your friend," Mathews said.

McCardy looked up at him. "Okay."

Laughton passed by McCardy. "Let's go," he said, continuing out of the room. His junior officer followed behind, and they let themselves out the front door. It was so dark beyond the house's aura, it was like they were on an island in space, disengaged from the rest of the world.

"A sister on the other side of the country and one name?" Mathews said, shutting off his body camera. "Half a name, really."

The pain in Laughton's face had returned, making it hard to see. "We're done for the night," he said, rubbing his head with both hands as he went to the truck. If only he could squeeze the pain away, out, gone. It made thinking impossible.

"Should I—?" Mathews started, as they got into the truck.

"I'm done," Laughton snapped, collapsing into the passenger seat. He closed his eyes before Mathews even hit the power button, and focused on his breathing, trying to breathe away the pain, just breathe. He was asleep before they'd left town.

C hief . . . Chief."

No, it was too early to get up. He could tell by the way his head felt, still stuffed with cotton, the left side of his face pulling everything down. Too early. In the mornings, he always felt better, something like optimistic about the day.

"Chief."

A rough hand on his shoulder. He opened his eyes just enough to glimpse the world, like dipping a toe into a pool to check the temperature before diving in. Shit. He was still in the truck. They were parked in the driveway of his house. All the lights were on inside. What time was it? Laughton sat up, rubbing his face.

"Chief, you all right?" Mathews said from the driver's seat.

"Yeah. Yeah. Fine." He took a deep breath and let it out through his nose. "I'm fine."

"I figured I should just drop you off. I'll take the truck home, and come pick you up in the morning."

Laughton nodded, taking the key fob from his pocket and dumping it in the cup holder. "Yeah. Okay. Yeah. See you to-morrow." He opened the passenger door.

"Six?"

"Make it six thirty," Laughton said getting out. He slammed the door, and Mathews pulled the truck out of the driveway as the chief went to his front door. He stood outside, closed his eyes, and counted to three. When he was younger, the first night of a murder investigation, he would go all night, driven in part by the chiding of his inexhaustible robot partner Kir. But right now, it was all he could do to keep standing. He tucked the last few hours away for the morning, grabbed the door handle, waiting for the chunky click of the lock disengaging as the knob verified his fingerprints, and then went inside.

"Daddy! Daddy! Daddy!" Erica pounded halfway down the stairs, completely nude. "Daddy, I carved a dolphin at recess by the twin trees."

Before he could respond to this overwhelming onslaught of noise, Betty breezed out of the kitchen. "No," she yelled. "No, no, no, no." She grabbed the banister and swung around, pointing a finger up the stairs. "No. You get in the bath," Betty yelled.

"Daddy!"

"Let your father get in the door. You do what you're supposed to be doing, and get in the bath."

"I was just—" Erica started, but Betty took one step up the stairs, and Erica spun around and scrambled up the stairs on all fours. The bathroom door closed but didn't latch.

Betty turned to Laughton. "Hello," she said, but it came out as almost an accusation instead of a greeting. Betty started for the kitchen. "I'm going to kill her," she said.

"What happened?" Laughton said, although he knew what happened. It happened almost every night. Dinner ended and then it was the nightly negotiation, do I have to take a bath, do I have to wash my hair, can I just rinse off with a wet washcloth, do I have to wash my hair, and once Erica was eventually upstairs, who knew what she did up there, ten, fifteen minutes before she even turned the water on, and now it was 8:43, and thirteen minutes after bedtime.

Laughton put his hand to his head. This wave of noise and anger was too much. He just needed a moment to himself to come in and unwind. Betty was in the kitchen, noisily putting dishes in the dishwasher. Laughton went in after her.

"I don't know what to do with her," Betty said without turning from the sink. "I'm so sick of this same bullshit. Why can't she just get ready for bed for once?" She turned her glare on him. "Is the water even on up there?"

"I don't know," he said.

"I'm going to—"

"I'll go check," Laughton said, holding his hands out in the same "calm down" gesture he used to settle abusive spouses, drunks, and the victims of crashes caused by people who refused to use the autopilot in their cars.

Betty stamped her foot, something Laughton still found adorable. Of course when Erica did it, Betty found it infuriating. "You just got home. You shouldn't need to deal with this. We've told her you need a breather when you get in."

"It's fine."

"It's not fine," Betty said. "Don't tell me it's fine."

"I don't know what you want me to say."

"Just agree with me."

That was too loaded to touch. Laughton went back through the living room and far enough up the stairs to hear that the water was still not running. "What are you doing up there, Erica!"

The water went on then. "Showering."

Laughton went back to the kitchen.

"Is the water on?" Betty said.

"Yes," he answered truthfully. No need to tell her it hadn't been until he called up.

"How was *your* day?" Betty said, but she said it angrily, like it was so unfair that he'd even had a day.

He pulled her to him, and she crossed her arms on her chest

between them, so that she was snuggling in as small a package as possible. She sighed and leaned in to him. Laughton enjoyed the moment of calm. His headache was full force again, and he was already thinking he couldn't get up tomorrow, he couldn't go to work.

"How's your head?" Betty mumbled into his chest.

"Bad," he said.

"I'm sorry."

"Me too," Laughton said.

Betty broke their hug now, and went to the cabinet where they kept the cookies. They were made by a pair of sisters in Beaufort in small batches when sugar was available. "You want one?" she asked, pulling a chocolate chip cookie out of the bag. Laughton just shook his head, going to the table, where he fell heavily into a chair.

"Want to hear how *my* day was?" Betty said, sitting across from him.

Laughton really just wanted to go upstairs, put Erica down, and collapse into bed, but he could see Betty needed to vent, and not just about bath time. "Marcos?"

"Marcos," she said.

Betty ran the Liberty Young Primary School, her brain-child, which she had founded and saw as the essential sister program to the Liberty Fertility Clinic, which she had also been instrumental in developing. Human schools had been almost nonexistent before the creation of the preserve. There had been a few isolated institutions in the cities, the only places where there were more than one or two human families. The attitude was that all that mattered was learning how to run a subsistence farm—a hydroponic vegetable garden, some fruit trees, a dairy cow or two, and all of the production therein. They needed these things to survive, and what was the good of anything else? Sure, there were some protein products made by entrepreneurial robots, and some grains—and sugar, of course, sugar—but most humans had no way of earning money, relying on government subsidies.

Betty believed that the establishment of the preserve was the beginning of a renewed human society, and that that required two essential components. The first and foremost was to increase the population. That was a project that was taking place all over the preserve, with a half dozen clinics in Charleston, and several clinics in the outer suburbs, all run by the pro-orgo group HOPS, the Human Organized Population Society. It was modeled on antique zoological preservation techniques that had been used to save specific animals from extinction—pandas, rhinos, tree frogs—animals that, in some cases, now outnumbered humans. The program comprised an enormous media campaign on television, in public transportation, and by door-to-door missionaries. All women were encouraged to conceive. The slogan was "A Baby in Every Belly." The clinics ran a sperm bank with artificial insemination, a sex match program for those who preferred the traditional method of conception, where genetically compatible individuals were coupled for assignations, and sex education for self-established pairs like the Laughtons. They also provided what prenatal and obstetric care could be gleaned from old medical textbooks and manuals, trying to increase the number of successful pregnancies and the infant survival rate.

The program had been slow to catch on, many people indifferent to the prospect of the human race's extinction, and some people outright opposed, believing that there would be no way to sustain a larger society with food production as inconsistent as it was. Betty spent a few hours at the clinic every afternoon, and then visited as many different women as she could, prospects she pursued like a salesman, making repeated visits, dragging Erica with her, almost as a sample, proof of concept.

The second component, and almost as important in Betty's view, was school. The bywords there were "teamwork," "compassion," "empathy," "resilience," and "social responsibility." The goal was to create good people who believed in the value of humanity and knew that survival was contingent on working together as one people. There were those that called it propaganda and inculcation, and who refused to participate. What was the point? Who even needed to know some of the subjects that were used as a medium—math, history, robotics—to teach fellowship? To the dissenters, agriculture and apathy and distraction equaled survival.

Betty's class was composed of six children who ranged in age from two to five, and one bad apple named Marcos, who threatened the chance for success of the experiment at all.

"I'm sorry to go on like that," she said, reaching her hand across the table and taking Laughton's. "You look like you're falling over."

Laughton knew he had to tell her about Smythe—it would be in the news soon, and she'd be angry at him for not sharing it with her—but he was worried she'd take it worse than he did, the waste of human life anathema to her. Then, without preamble, he said, "There's been a murder."

Betty pulled her hand back, like she'd touched something hot, or maybe something disgusting, and blinked rapidly. "What do you mean?"

"Someone's been killed. Behind Kramer's."

Her head fell back, her face pointing to the ceiling, eyes closed. Then she looked back at him. "And you had to listen to me talk about a damn brat. Why didn't you say something?"

"I just did."

"Goddamn it. Do you know who did it?"

He shook his head. The movement sent a shot of pain across his cheeks. He must have winced, because standing up, Betty said, "You better get to sleep. You don't want to start the day still dragging today's headache with you."

"Yeah."

"And you better catch the son of a bitch."

Just then, Erica ran into the room, her hair dripping water, soaking the shoulders of her pajama top, turning the baby pink to almost magenta. She jumped on Laughton's lap.

"Erica, you need to ask first," Betty chastised.

Laughton wrapped his arms around his daughter; she was so skinny, he engulfed her. She flopped on his lap, the top of her head hitting his cheek. The pain was explosive, and he released her, nearly throwing her off his lap. "Fuck," he said.

"Erica, you've got to be careful!" Betty said.

Laughton held his hand to his face. His shirt was soaking wet where Erica's hair had been pressed to his chest.

"I'm sorry," Erica said. She looked as though she was about to cry.

"It's fine," he said, placing a caring hand on the top of her head. "It's fine. Let's go to bed."

She wrapped her arms around his right hand in anxiety, almost hanging on his arm. Usually he would have forced her to let go—she was hurting him—but tonight he dragged her along, Betty trailing behind them. This was his family.

Erica tried to pull him onto the bed as he tucked her in, but he knew if he even sat, he wouldn't be able to get up again. He kissed her wet temple, and said, "I love you, beautiful."

"Stay," she said, gripping his hand tighter.

"I've got to go to sleep," he said.

"Erica, let go," Betty said. "I'll sit with you for a minute."

Erica didn't let go, but Laughton wrenched his hand free, the action causing him to tighten the muscles in his face, which made his stomach turn with the pain. He stumbled out of the room, almost tripping into his room and onto the bed, where he collapsed. There was something he was forgetting to do, like the slipup in the interview at the supermarket, forgetting to try to establish a timeline. But what was he missing?

All he could do was breathe, trying to control the pain, to sleep.

———

The rising and falling tinkle of notes penetrated the chief's sleep, and he was slowly aware his thigh was buzzing, an odd vibration that made him feel as though he needed to pee. He opened his eyes. The room was dark. He was mostly on the bed, his legs protruding over the edge from the knees down, and he was still dressed. His phone. In his pocket.

He rolled over, reaching into his jeans.

Betty uncurled herself from the small corner of bed that had been left to her once Laughton had collapsed. "Make it stop," she mumbled as, still asleep, she swung her feet over the edge of the bed and started to shuffle to the bathroom. "Stop," she moaned.

Laughton sat up and looked at his phone's bright display, squinting at the light. At least it didn't hurt, his facial pain and headache having retreated to little more than an annoyance, thank god. The name displayed there, however, squeezed everything in his chest—"Kir." Only one reason *he'd* be calling. Someone must have talked, and the news of the murder had gotten out. Maybe Laughton didn't have to answer it. He could claim to have missed it. But that would only make it worse later. He swiped to pick up the call.

"Hey, lazybones," Kir said. "Sleeping on the job?"

Laughton wasn't in the mood. "I'm not on the job."

"The job is always on," Kir said. "You know that."

Kir had been Laughton's first, and only, partner during his seventeen years on the Baltimore City Police Department. A series fourteen, class five robot, Kir was superior to humans in every way: intelligence, strength, stamina, senses. Unlike most robots, however, Kir had a great respect for humans, no small part of that due to Laughton.

"What do you want, Kir?" Laughton said, not masking the annoyance in his voice.

"Help," Kir said. He paused. "Didn't see that one coming, huh?"

Betty shuffled back into the bedroom. "Go 'way," she mumbled. She wouldn't have any memory of the episode in the morning.

Laughton got up, and left the room, finding his way down the stairs blindly. "How'd you know I caught a body," Laughton said. His stomach sunk. "Don't tell me it hit the news."

Silence.

It lasted long enough that Laughton said, "Kir?"

"I didn't," the robot said at last. "When?"

"Why'd you wake me up, then?" Laughton said. He went into the kitchen and turned on the light. It made the window over the sink a mirror. Tufts of hair stood up on the sides of his head, his clothes were wrinkled. At least it wasn't a video call. He didn't need to give Kir more fodder.

"I was calling to ask *you* to help *me*," Kir said. Laughton knew the tone. His partner was serious. "But—"

"What you got?" Laughton said, bracing himself for it.

"Jesse, if you've got a homicide, we need to let Secretary Pattermann know. Do you know—"

"I know."

"Do you know what people are going to do when they hear there was a murder on the preserve?" Kir said. "This is exactly the excuse the anti-preserve groups are looking for."

"I know."

"I'm coming down there. I—"

"Kir, I know," Laughton said. "That's why I'm keeping it quiet. I'm going to solve this before anyone has a chance to claim we can't take care of our own problems. I need to take care of it *myself*. Now tell me why you called, or let me get to sleep."

"Robocides," Kir said. "Five of them."

"What does the HHS have to do with dead robots?" Kir was the expert on human crime for the Department of Health and Human Services, the federal unit that oversaw the preserve system. He had tried to bring Laughton with him, but just as Kir had jumped at the chance to work at the federal level, Laughton had jumped at the chance to leave robots behind and control his own department. "Isn't that the opposite of your jurisdiction?"

"Sims," Kir said. "Seems like they were all users. Hit by some new program that wipes the robot before he can upload. Plug and play and die. Rumor is that the sim originated on the preserve, so, the cases've come to me. Or at least, I've been called in. There are plenty of other cops working it."

Sims. Jesse thought of all those sticks at Smythe's house. "Kir, my body is a sims hacker."

Silence again. At last, "Shit."

"Coincidence," Jesse said, not believing it for a second.

"Look, everyone knows the preserve is a sims distribution ground. I was calling you to try to get ahead of this, but if you've got a dead hacker within days of a deadly sim hitting the street, robots are going to be all over the preserve."

"We don't want the department on the preserve, Kir."

"Honestly, we don't want to come in either, but it won't be just the department unless we move fast. You're right, it's better for everyone if the preserve can handle itself. But I was already worried the dead robots were going to lead to you. If this homicide is connected . . ."

"So you wanted eyes on the ground?"

"That was the idea. But now I'm coming, whether you want it or not, as soon as I tell Grace Pattermann so she can begin damage control. If you and I work this, maybe we'll be able to control it."

"Who says I can't do that on my own?"

"Jesse, let's help each other."

The tone was sincere. Even if they couldn't read emotions that well, they could emulate them pretty accurately. Laughton knew he would say yes. It would be so much better to have Kir at his side than Dunrich or even Mathews. But he wasn't going to give the robot the satisfaction just yet. "It's late, Kir. Let's talk about it in the morning."

"Sure," Kir said.

"Sure?" Laughton hadn't expected that.

"Sure. I'll see you in the morning," Kir said. "Say hi to Betty and Erica." And the robot hung up.

Laughton looked at the phone in his hand. "Sure." If he could read Kir, his ex-partner could read him. Kir knew the answer was going to be yes. And to his surprise, Laughton was looking forward to it.

D ad."

"Oh, my god, Jesus," Laughton gasped, flipping around on the bed, wild fear flooding his chest. Erica was leaning against the mattress. "You scared the— You scared me."

"Mom said to wake you up," she said. She was already dressed. "Mr. Mathews is outside."

He looked toward his nightstand for his phone, and Erica handed it to him. The face lit up: 6:35. He'd slept late. "Okay," he said. "I'm up."

"Can we play a game?" Erica said.

Laughton threw back the covers, and started to rise, but Erica was in his way. "Excuse me," he said, and she moved to let him up. "We can't play right now. I've got to get ready."

"Can't you get ready after I go to school?"

"You're going to be leaving in twenty minutes anyway," he said, on his way to the bathroom. "Go downstairs, I'll be right down."

"We could play for just five minutes," she said.

"Did I answer you?" he said, annoyed. "Go downstairs." He went into the bathroom and closed the door. He raised the seat of the toilet, and heard Erica clomp down the stairs. Every night he felt guilty that he couldn't give Erica what she needed, that he wasn't a fun dad, that he wasn't an empathetic dad, that the message he always sent was that he was annoyed, and that he was unavailable. But then right from the first thing in the morning, the barrage of requests, of questions, ignoring the answers, pushing, and the annoyance bubbled up right from the start of the day. She'd be gone in twenty minutes. He could play with her that long, he thought.

Downstairs, however, Betty was standing at the door, her bag already over her shoulder, watching Erica, who was on the floor putting her shoes on. "Hey," she said.

He went to kiss her, and she returned it with a chaste peck on the lips like a social nicety, devoid of feeling. "Are you angry at me?" he said.

"No. It's just been a morning," she said. "Come on, Erica."

"You said to make sure my shoes were tied tightly. I'm triple-knotting them."

Betty's lips got thin. It didn't require expertise to see her anger. She turned to Laughton. "I've got the clinic this afternoon."

"Okay."

"Who called in the middle of the night?"

Laughton looked out the door, and waved to Mathews to come in from the truck. "Kir. He's coming."

Betty's head snapped around, and she fixed him with large eyes. "He's not staying here, is he?"

Laughton hadn't thought about that. "I don't think so. I don't know. Maybe. Is that a problem?"

"No, of course, it's just, I'm tired, I don't feel like hosting. Is this the . . . case from yesterday?"

Erica jumped up. "Ready," she said, throwing herself against Laughton, wrapping her arms around his waist, and hooking her feet around his leg. "Uncle Kir is coming to visit!"

"Erica. Get down," Betty said.

"Yes," Laughton said.

"Yay!"

"Erica!" Betty snapped.

"Call me," Laughton said, physically prying his daughter off of him. "We'll talk later."

Betty opened the storm door.

"Goodbye, have fun," Laughton said as Erica bounded out the front door, nearly crashing into Mathews.

"Call me," Betty said as she walked out the door. "Morning, Jim."

"Betty," Mathews said.

The younger officer came inside. "Ready, Chief?" he said.

"Give me five minutes," Laughton said. Upstairs, Laughton entertained the wishful thought that he could just get back in bed, but instead he brushed his teeth and changed his shirt. At least his head didn't hurt. The beginning of the day was always the best time for Laughton, and it usually filled him with hope and a sense that life was manageable.

As they drove to the station, Laughton tried to run through the normal order of things in a homicide, certain he was missing something, but his mind remained blank. He half expected a loitering handful of reporters at the station, but there was no one. It meant everyone'd kept quiet about it for the last fourteen hours, even the Kramer's people, something that seemed impossible. He wondered how long the vacuum would last. He needed to make the most of it.

When the preserve system was being developed, there had been a long debate about policing and jurisdiction. Most robots saw the preserve as a way to rid themselves of the human "problem." They were more than content to let the preserve have its own justice system. Robot law enforcement, however, despite the fact that they had always employed a small number of human officers—Laughton having been one of them—and could therefore, when being open-minded, vouch for their competence, still wanted to have final jurisdiction. They knew that crime would not obey borderlines, and that there would no doubt be a flow of criminal activities onto and off of the preserve, and they didn't want to accept any limits on their power.

In the end, a small list of crimes was designated as federal offenses, giving jurisdiction to the FBI with mandated oversight by the Department of Health and Human Services: sim trafficking, abduction/missing persons, and cybernetic crimes. Murder had been included on many of the early proposed lists, pushed for by the human population, who assumed, without good evidence, that most murderers would be robots. To pass the bill, however, murder was struck from the list, seen by the federal government as a strictly human problem. Robots just didn't care. Humans were assured unofficially that any crime perpetrated by a robot on preserve land would fall under the purview of the FBI and that preserve law enforcement could expect federal assistance.

Laughton knew that this murder would be a test case. Many who had lobbied for the federal designation of murder would use Smythe as a rallying call. It wouldn't help that there was the possible connection to sim trafficking, or that the use of a Taser might point to a robot assailant, both cases that would mandate FBI involvement. On the robot side, the more militant contingent in law enforcement wanted any excuse to invalidate many of the protections of the preserve by moving in as a standing army or rescinding the preserve altogether.

At his desk, Laughton opened the video chat on his tablet, and added Beaufort police chief Tommy Tantino, Georgetown chief of police Al Bell, and Commissioner Ontero to the invitation list. They needed to coordinate a manhunt for Jones and, more importantly, how they were going to handle the politicians and the press once this went live. There would be tremendous pressure to wrap up the case quickly while most of the country waited for the police department's failure. His finger hovered over the call button. What was he going to tell them, though? It would be better if he had something to show that the investigation was advancing before he talked to them. Leave them deniability a little longer until he could provide some sound bites. He let his finger linger long enough to become uncomfortable, and then pulled his hand away. He yelled, "Mathews!"

Mathews appeared in the doorway.

"Call Dunrich also," the chief said.

Mathews looked over his shoulder. "Dunrich. Come here." He stepped into the office, and Dunrich stepped in behind him. The officers stood just inside the door, unwilling to commit a full entrance, like infrequent offenders called in to the principal. Laughton took a moment to consider the entire Liberty police force stuffed into a room that would have served as a maintenance closet at the Baltimore PD headquarters, where he used to work. It made him feel very small-town, and not in the good way he'd enjoyed over the last nine months. God, they hadn't even made it a full year.

His men shifted their weight from one foot to the other, waiting in silence.

"You get anything from the interviews at the supermarket?"

Dunrich shook his head. "Nobody saw anything. Most people had never been behind the market ever."

"Anyone seem off?"

"Chief, every single person said almost the same thing, and half of them were people I recognized. Nobody knew anything."

Laughton nodded.

"I need to call Beaufort, Georgetown, and the commissioner," he said, pointing to the tablet sitting on his desk, "hopefully before the press hears about it. But I want to have more than half a name when I do. If we can get out in front of this thing, maybe even catch the guy, we'll avoid a mess of trouble far bigger than one dead hacker."

Dunrich looked at his feet while Mathews chewed his lip. They wanted orders.

Laughton tried to think. What was their play? Find Jones, of course. Find anyone else Smythe might have known; he came to town to shop, they should check the bars, women, that meant the clinic . . . Maybe see if McCardy had thought of anything once he'd calmed—

Oh, shit. McCardy. He'd already fucked up. He jumped up. "We need to get back out to the house," he said. "Idiot! We should have brought McCardy in last night. He could be a target. Dunrich, we need a better picture of Smythe's life. Check the bars, the café, anywhere he might stop when he comes through Liberty. Mathews, you're with me. We'll take two cars. One of us should stay out there. Jones might show up."

They waited for more.

"Go!"

Dunrich left. The sound of the outer door closing on its pneumatic hinges marked his exit.

Damn headache. He couldn't believe he hadn't posted someone there last night. He had wanted to get home so badly, the possibility that McCardy could be a target too hadn't occurred to him. What other rookie mistakes had he made in his nightly funk?

He grabbed his tablet, and rounded his desk, Mathews backing out of the office to clear the way. "Did you manage to get ahold of Smythe's sister?" he asked as they headed for the door.

Mathews shook his head. "The number McCardy gave me didn't work, and I haven't been able to find anything about her online. No social media, nothing."

"Great."

Outside, the patrol car was gone. Laughton went to his truck as Mathews got into his own car. Laughton called up McCardy and Smythe's house in the truck's memory, and hit go. The truck began to back out of the spot.

Had nine months really made him this inept?

He looked at his tablet and saw Ontero's name on the screen.

The autopsy! He erased Ontero's name and called Dunrich.

"Dunrich."

"What happened to the body?" Laughton said.

"Went to the hospital in Charleston. Nowhere else to keep a body."

Then they were really lucky it hadn't hit the news. "I better get down there."

"You want me to go, Chief?"

"No. Bars. Liquor stores. Talk to everyone." He hung up without waiting for a response.

He punched in Ontero's personal cell phone number. It rang once and then Ontero's voice filled the car. "Ontero."

"Chris, it's Jesse."

"What do you need?" the commissioner said.

"Know the name of the medical examiner?"

"Why do you need a medical examiner?" his voice cautious.

"We sent a body down yesterday."

"Homicide?"

"Looks like it."

"Shit. Shit. Shit. Shit."

"That about says it," Laughton said.

"I don't know who the fuck the medical examiner is. I don't even know if we have one."

"Can you find out for me? I'm on my way to the victim's house. Tell whoever it is to wait for me for the autopsy."

"You should have called me yesterday."

"I was a little busy."

"Damn it, Jesse."

"Oh, I need a computer team too. Vic was a hacker. Need someone to go through his computers."

"Tell me you know who did this?"

"I have no idea," Laughton said.

"Well, find the fuck out."

"Get me those computer techs and an ME."

The phone went dead. Ontero'd hung up.

Laughton took the truck off of auto, and gave it gas, impatient with the speed.

McCardy better not be dead.

hief Laughton manually parked the car across the street from the hackers' house. Mathews pulled up behind him. A two-door, orange microcar that had not been there the night before was in front of the house.

Laughton got out of the truck, and Mathews joined him. "Someone's here," Mathews said.

"Maybe McCardy had a friend come stay with him. Didn't want to be alone after his best friend was murdered."

"He said he didn't know anyone else."

"Well, here we go," Laughton said.

A man in a black collarless T-shirt and a sky-blue jacket came around the side of the house. He was tall, Laughton estimated at least six foot two, with a well-groomed beard trimmed close to his face.

Laughton started to cross the street. "Excuse me!" he called. "Excuse me."

The man froze, then took a half step back, as though he was going to retreat, only to stop himself, and took a step forward.

Laughton was on him now. Mathews went and immediately stood behind the man and to the side.

"I'm just walking here," the man said.

"Guy whose house it is know you're walking here?" Laughton said. He pushed a button on his body cam, and his phone buzzed. He looked at it, and it showed a picture of the man, but without a beard. "Carter Jones," Laughton said, reading the name off the face recognition ID.

"No shit," Mathews said.

"We're looking for a Jones."

eyebrows down and together, both eyelids narrowed, chin pulled back—concern

"Why?"

"You friends with the people who own the house?"

"Yeah," Jones said, trying to figure out what the police wanted. "Did I do anything, Officers?"

"You're going to tell us. But first, let's see if your friend is home."

"No answer. That's why I was around the back. To see if there was another way in."

No answer, Laughton thought. He didn't like that. "Come on," he said.

Jones hesitated, but Mathews poked him in the back, and the sims dealer walked forward. The police flanked him.

They went to the front door. The outlay of black solar panels sucked in the light, leaving not even a reflection of the sky, just a harsh, hard darkness that stripped away any sense of being in the natural world, the grass beneath all dead or dying.

The chief knocked. "Body camera," he said.

"Already on," Mathews said.

Laughton knocked again.

"Was there anything out back?" Mathews said.

Jones shook his head.

The chief went back to the truck and retrieved a crowbar. At the door, he handed the crowbar to Mathews, letting the younger officer fit it into the space between the door and the jamb. Mathews pulled back, and the doorjamb splintered. He reset it and applied more force, causing the wood to crack further, then he put his shoulder against the door and it popped open.

The whirring of the computer fans met them, and nothing else. "Mr. McCardy!" Laughton called.

There was no answer.

He pushed Jones in ahead of him. Inside, he pointed to the stairs, and Mathews started up while Laughton headed back to the room where they had spoken to McCardy the day before, herding Jones before him. It was deserted. He continued through the kitchen and out to a little sunroom off the back of the house. No one was there either. The backyard was fenced in by a six-foot-high wooden fence. The back gate was open. The rear of the house from the neighboring street was visible through a sparse stand of trees.

Laughton went back to the room where the hackers' workstations were set up just as Mathews came in shaking his head. "Nothing."

Laughton pointed to a door in the kitchen. "Check the basement."

Mathews crossed to the door. Laughton examined the desk where McCardy had sat last night. Jones had wandered over to the shelf of memory sticks. He reached for one, and Laughton said, "Don't touch anything. It's all evidence."

"Evidence of what?" Jones said.

Laughton didn't bother to answer, continuing to examine the desk. One of the screens showed a distorted, wide-angle view of the front of the house. They had cameras, but if McCardy was telling the truth about Smythe's programming, if they tried to access any recordings, the whole place would probably burn down. It'd have to wait for the tech team.

Mathews returned from the basement. "Place is empty."

"Shit," Laughton said. "The idiot must have panicked." He damned himself again for not leaving someone posted the night before. That should have been automatic. Now they'd lost the one person they *knew* knew Smythe well.

"Guess Jones is in the clear," Mathews said. "He'd be pretty stupid to come here if he'd killed Smythe."

"Wait, what?" Jones said.

jaw dangling, eyes wide—surprise

"Someone killed Carl? Carl's dead."

"Unless he was coming to kill McCardy," Laughton said, "and that's why McCardy ran."

"Whoa, whoa, whoa, what are you saying?"

head tilted, eyes narrowed, brows lowered—suspicion

The surprise had been genuine, the suspicion natural. Seemed like Jones genuinely didn't know Smythe was dead.

"Is Carl really dead?" Jones said. He ran his hand over the top of his head. "What the fuck?"

"Let's take this outside." They led him to the curb, and had him sit down. His leg was jiggling with nerves.

"What the hell are you going to do with me?" he said.

"You're not under arrest, if that's what you're asking," Laughton said.

"Under arrest? For what? Check me." He held his arms out to either side as though he expected to be frisked right then. "Check my car. No sims. No memory sticks. Nothing." He let his arms fall. Then his eyebrows crumpled into a groove above his nose as he realized. "You don't mean Carl?" He scoffed. "You think I killed Carl?" Jones stood up then. Tall as he was, he probably wasn't used to looking up to talk to someone. "I didn't. You've got to believe me."

"Then tell us who did."

"How would I know?"

Laughton held up his phone, and read, "Carter Jones, six counts of sims possession, two with greater than twenty sticks." He looked at Jones. "Given that you're a sims dealer, and Smythe wrote sims, and you showed up at his house the day after he was killed says to me, you probably have a very good idea of who killed him."

"You need to help me," Jones said.

"Why do you need help?"

"Hello? They killed Carl. And where's Sam? What happened to Sam?"

"Who's 'they'?"

"Do you really know shit?" He looked around for someone to share his incredulity, but was met with blank faces.

"Who killed Smythe?" Laughton said. "Do you know? Maybe we can protect you if we know the people to go after."

" '*Maybe*,' " he sneered. "At least you're being honest."

Laughton shifted his weight. "Mr. Jones. I know you're scared, but unless you tell me what's going on, I don't know what I can do for you."

Jones closed his eyes and put his fingertips to his temples, talking to himself. "This fucking app." An edge of panic had entered his voice. He opened his eyes. "Fuck!"

At the word "app," Laughton's stomach seized. If Kir's case *was* connected, the shit would really hit the fan.

"What app?" Mathews said.

Jones focused on Laughton. "My *job* is the hackers. My job is to protect the hackers, because I'm the *only* one who knows them. But if someone got to Smythe and now Sam's gone, what do you think that'll do to my reputation? And worse, what if they want to get to me so they can get to my other hackers?"

"Why would anyone be killing hackers?" Laughton said.

Jones's shoulders fell, and he swallowed.

Dropping the pose revealed that he was much younger than Laughton had at first thought, maybe twenty-six at oldest. The beard was deceptive.

Jones shook his head. "You really don't know shit, do you?" he said.

Laughton noted the inner corners of his eyebrows raise in sadness.

"You haven't heard about the killer app? I thought it was all over the news."

"Hot shots killing robots," Laughton said.

"Yes. Thank you. God."

"What?" Mathews said. "Someone want to fill me in?"

"You're sure it's connected?" Laughton said. "You're certain?"

"No, but . . ."

"But what!"

"It just—what if it is?"

Laughton remembered what McCardy had said the night before about his partner's work. Computers actually burning down. These robots melting from a program? Of course it was connected.

The dealer's hand was shaking uncontrollably at his side.

tucked chin, the mouth stretched wide toward the ears— panic

Laughton knew the amorphous fear that victims' friends and family felt after a murder. Off balance, generalized apprehension. This was more specific. "You know who did it," he said.

Jones looked at him. There was a flash, a micro-expression, a fraction of a second that showed remorse before defensiveness replaced it. "What? No."

He felt guilty about something. "What are you afraid of?" Laughton said.

"I told you."

"What are you afraid of?"

"What? Nothing. It's just, if people start pointing fingers at me . . . But maybe somebody thinks they know who wrote the code, and if it was Sam and Smythe . . ."

Laughton's whole face felt heavy, as though his visage was going to slough off. "Who!" he snapped.

"Look," Jones said. "I'm not saying it makes sense. Maybe they're not connected, but all I know is that I was Sam and Smythe's middleman, and I don't know if that puts me in the line of fire. I came to find out what Sam knew about the robots who got burned, but it's too late for that. Fuck."

Jones had regained his sense of outrage. Whatever he was suppressing was gone. Laughton tried to think. He asked Jones, "How many hackers do you handle?"

"Six, no, seven. But you're crazy if you think I'll give up their names."

"All on the preserve? Outside of Charleston?"

"Yes."

"So you pick up the memory sticks. Then what?"

Jones hesitated, his eyes going up, searching for an answer.

"You know what," Laughton said. "Fuck it, you *are* under arrest."

"What! No! The Sisters."

"Like nuns?" Mathews said, and laughed.

"The Sisters," Jones said. "They get the product off the preserve. Pack it in with their produce, and then I don't know where, out to stupid metals who like to fuck with their brains." Seeing the next question, he said, "They run a farm."

"Okay," Laughton said, trying to get his head around it all—dead robots, farmers. Jones looked like he was ready to bolt, his fear growing as he stood there. For talking? "Sure you had nothing to do with those hot shots?"

"Why the fuck would I want to mess up my business? Use your brain, man."

Laughton thought, If only he *could* use his brain. If only it didn't feel so far away. He wished he could just plug in a memory stick and fix his head.

"You're coming back to Liberty with us," the chief said.

"Like hell I am."

"Like hell you are," Laughton said, and Mathews grabbed Jones's upper right arm.

"You wanted help. Come with us. We'll protect you."

"I don't know, man," Jones said.

Laughton flexed his jaw. "Mr. Jones, I know you're scared, but think for a minute. Forget whoever's killing hackers, or sims, or any of that. We've got a murder on the preserve. We don't come up with a killer, and the robots are going to use it as an excuse to come in here and take over the investigation. And then how long before they're claiming we need robots on the preserve as peacekeepers, and then this whole place is an open-air prison instead of a wildlife preserve. You think they're going to ignore the sims traffic the way we do? Like you said, who cares if the robots want to fuck themselves up, but if we don't close this up fast, they're going to fuck us all up, and then you can forget about sims."

The part of Jones's face that could be seen above his beard had gone splotchy, whites and reds. He pulled his arm from Laughton's grip. "How do I know it wasn't you guys killed Carl?"

"Two of us . . . ," Mathews said.

Jones whipped around at the sound of Mathews's voice.

"And one of you. If we were going to kill you, you'd be dead."

Jones looked back to Laughton.

The chief knew the dealer hadn't really thought the police were dangerous. But he didn't trust them either. Laughton could see him weighing his options: police protection or running.

"You leave the preserve, how safe are you going to be?" Laughton said.

Jones pulled his shoulders in. His eyes turned toward the ground. He was withdrawing.

"Just help us out with a couple names and addresses—"

"You're asking me to kill myself?" Jones said without looking at Laughton.

"Not if you're with us. We will protect you."

Jones started to shake his head. "Nah," he said, "no." He stepped back. "Forget this," he said, and turned toward his car.

Mathews reached for him, but Laughton held Mathews back.

"No," Jones said, walking sideways to his car, so he was half facing them. "I'm not under arrest. I'm not sticking around."

"You're making a mistake," Laughton said. "We can't protect you if we don't know where you are."

He was at his car now. "You can't protect me if you *know* where I am," he said, opening the driver's-side door and getting in. "Ask around about the Sisters. That's all I'm going to say." He got in the car and slammed the door.

Mathews took a step toward the car as it came alive.

"No," Laughton said. "He'll be more useful as bait. We'll track the car."

"Won't he figure that?"

Laughton watched the sims dealer as the car drove away. Jones's face was stricken. "He won't be thinking straight long enough for it to occur to him. Start recording the scene in there." Laughton nodded at the house. "3-D scans, catalog everything. Ontero's already sending Computer Forensics in from Charleston to start digging through the mess of servers in there, and I want you here when they get here. I'll head back and see what I can find out about these Sisters."

Mathews's jaw tightened.

"You don't agree with letting him go. Soon, I might not either. But we had nothing to hold him on anyway."

"Sure we did. A laundry list."

Laughton nodded. "Let me know if you find anything."

By the time Laughton made it back to Liberty, he'd exhausted every database he could access looking for the
Sisters. It was just too common a word, and with nothing more to go on, he couldn't bring up anything in the system
that seemed right. He was thinking over next steps when he
heard Dunrich laughing, and his tension turned to anger.
The officer was leaning far back in his desk chair in hysterics.
Manuel Guthrie was in the slatted, wooden chair to the side of
Dunrich's desk. He was holding out his phone for Dunrich to
see. Whatever had the officer in hysterics was displayed there.
Kara Letts was at her news desk on the muted flat-panel TV
on the wall. The closed captions said something about garbage
dumps. At least Kara had other things than homicide to get
people worked up about.

Dunrich sat up suddenly when he caught sight of Laughton, his chair almost rolling away with him. He grabbed his
desk and pulled himself in. Manuel Guthrie turned to see what
had spooked his friend. "Chief," Guthrie said.

"What the hell are you doing here?" he said, ignoring
Manny. "You're supposed to be out canvassing."

Guthrie held his phone out to the chief, trying to run interference for his friend. "Check this out."

"Another time, Manny," Laughton said. He wasn't in the
mood for any humor. He raised his eyebrows at Dunrich.

"I did canvass," Dunrich said, his eyes not meeting the
chief's. "Nobody knew anything."

"You canvassed the whole town in two and a half hours? Everyone?"

"You just said the bars."

"Show some initiative! Anyone, everyone. Did you even ask Manny?"

"I don't know nothing about anything, Chief," Manny said.

"I'll go now," Dunrich said.

"Damn right you'll go now. You— No, just wait." He needed to get to this autopsy. Time was just draining. "Did you at least find out who the ME is?"

"I—"

"That's a no," Laughton said. "And you've got nothing better to do than sit around joking?" He threw his hands up with a "God!" and went to his office. He sat behind his desk and rubbed his forehead. Who'd he know in electronic narco who might know who the Sisters were?

Before he could even reach for his tablet, Dunrich called from the front of the station, "Chief! You want to see this!"

Laughton jumped up, yelling, "Fucking Dunrich," heading out of his office, but Laughton's attention was already on the television screen. The sound was on now, the closed captions a few paces behind. The commissioner stood at a lectern outside Charleston Police headquarters with the preserve governor and the mayor of Charleston flanking him. Two other figures stood just behind them. One—a small woman in narrow red glasses, black hair pulled back in a loose ponytail—Laughton recognized immediately: Kir's boss, Grace Pattermann, secretary of the Department of Health and Human Services. Her presence as a representative of the federal government was worrisome, but it was the other participant that had Laughton's attention: a seven-foot, uniformed military robot called Colonel Brandis. The sight made

Laughton's stomach drop. Here was the nightmare, a robotic intervention, and Brandis the worst possible representative, a seventy-year-old robot of the old guard, and one of the most vocal anti-orgos in the world.

Laughton realized he was holding his breath, and forced air into his lungs. The on-screen text read "Homicide Sims Connection." Damn! This was the opposite of keeping the investigation quiet. The commissioner was saying they had multiple leads, and nobody had to worry. As though Brandis and Pattermann weren't reasons to worry on their own. He went on to say there was no evidence that suggested robot involvement. The text switched to "Robots Not Involved." The robot government had sent a delegation to assist and consult only.

At least they weren't publicly linking Smythe's death to the virus that was killing robots. There was that, at least.

"Fuck," he said. He turned and saw Dunrich just standing at his desk. "Get on the phone," he said. "Find out about that autopsy."

Dunrich sat down quickly and grabbed his phone. Laughton felt a little guilty for taking out his anger on Dunrich.

The outside door opened, but Laughton started for his office without waiting to see who it was. He hadn't gotten around his desk, however, when Kir walked through his office door. Six foot with dark hair, protruding cheekbones, and sunken cheeks, Kir was an imposing figure who could pass as human. On the preserve, where no one expected a robot, most people wouldn't even realize he wasn't human until they spent a little time with him. "This is it?" the robot said.

Laughton was surprised by the smile he could feel spread across his face. He felt lighter. "Son of a bitch, it's good to see you," he said, and stepped forward. The old partners hugged. It was always disconcerting how cool a robot was to the touch. It made Laughton feel ridiculous, this upwelling of feelings.

"It's dead in here," Kir said.

"Only have two officers."

"I saw the one on the phone. The other's out in the clown car?"

"Fuck you," Laughton said, noticing his language, the cursing around Kir. It reminded him there was a reason why he had left. Kir was a bad influence. That had nothing to do with whether or not he was a robot.

"Sit down," Kir said.

Laughton tried not to bristle at being given an order in his own office. There were a lot of reasons he had left Baltimore, and it didn't take long, apparently, to remember what they were. Kir might have considered himself pro-orgo—he voted for the preserve, solved human cases no one else would, didn't mod his body, and now worked for the Department of Health and Human Services—but it was impossible for him to not still carry an intrinsic attitude of superiority.

Laughton felt the ire rankle across his shoulders, his muscles tightening, but he tried to not let it get to him. It was just Kir. The thought filled him with exhaustion, and there was a wave of pain through his face.

Kir caught it, the thousands and thousands of hours of Laughton's face recorded in his memory giving the robot the ability to read his ex-partner that far exceeded most robots' abilities, even Kir's own abilities to read other humans. "Pain still bad?"

Laughton nodded. "Yeah."

"And my niece?"

"Perfect," Laughton said.

"So where are we?"

"I was just about to go to Charleston to see the postmortem."

"How long has it been since you found the body?"

"Fuck you. I've been busy."

"I wasn't saying anything."

"You were, and I don't want to hear it," Laughton said.

"Hear what?" Kir played innocent.

"Kir, this whole thing's such a goddamn mess."

"You don't know the half of it," Kir said.

"I saw Brandis."

"Let's go. You can finish filling me in on the way, and then I'll fill you in."

They went back out to the squad room, and Kara Letts was talking to an anonymous hacker over an open phone line on the TV. Laughton had a moment of regret at having let Jones go, just when the man might have identified the caller. He snapped at Dunrich and pointed at the television. "Find out who she's talking to," he said.

Dunrich started to hang up his phone, then put it back to his ear, unsure if he was supposed to keep after the autopsy or drop it for this new thing.

"When you're finished," Laughton said.

On the television, Kara Letts was asking the hacker, "Did you ever worry about your safety before the preserve?"

"No," the voice of the hacker said. "I'm not saying I'm worried now . . ."

At least someone was thinking straight.

Outside, Kir said, "How have you been, though? The family? What's life on the ground like here?"

"Until yesterday, boring."

"That bad, huh?"

"I don't know that it's a bad thing. It is what it is." He let them into the car. "How are things at the federal level?"

"Have you seen the killer app?"

"What do you mean, have I seen it?" He punched "The University of South Carolina Medical Center" into the GPS.

"It's pretty horrifying, the pictures. Just burnt and melted plastic and metal."

"Isn't it a DOJ problem?"

"They think it came from the preserve, so . . ."

Laughton thought of everything he'd learned about Smythe so far. "Yeah, well I think that's why my man got killed."

"And that's why I'm here," Kir said.

"Got any leads?"

"Maybe," Kir said. "Our first body was fifty-two hours ago. There've been at least five total. All had ported sims, the same red memory stick."

"When you say 'body,' what do you mean? They're robots."

"This sim fries their hard drives, literally. The memory, the operating system, completely burned out." A slight pause. "Check your phone," Kir said as Laughton's phone buzzed.

Laughton looked. "Shit." It was an autopsy photo, the access panel at the back of a robot's head was open, revealing a black melted mess inside. "Shit."

"You swipe, you can see the memory stick."

Laughton swiped to the next photo: a simple, undistinguished red memory stick, about the size of a thumbnail. It didn't match any of the ones he'd seen at Sam and Smythe's. He handed the phone back to Kir.

"Plug-and-play sims have been growing in popularity over the last year or two. They run automatically, no chance to scan for a virus. Junkies like the unpredictability, the abandonment. The risk is real, it turns out."

"I don't want it to be true, but my vic is your man."

"What do you know?"

"Smythe's partner said that he'd developed safeguards for his computers: if anyone tries to hack in, the machine fries, literally."

They sat in silence for a moment, considering the implications.

"Then it's damn good I'm here," Kir said.

"And I just fucking let his middleman go," Laughton said. "We've got his car info, and he wasn't going to tell me shit, so I thought it might be nice to see where he went."

"Look, we work the case. With humans, it can always be personal, even with all of the other stuff swirling around."

"Personal," Laughton said. He grabbed the wheel and disengaged the auto-drive, pulling the car over.

"What?"

Laughton nodded toward the building across the street. "Let's see if it's personal."

The Liberty Fertility Clinic was located in what had long ago been an enormous house. It was three stories high with thick white columns holding a veranda above the entrance. A porch wrapped around the side. A sign in the front yard, rising out of a well-kept hedge, announced the clinic's name and hours, but nowhere on the house proper was its current use apparent. It seemed an appropriate building for the propagation of the human race, a house harkening to a time of human splendor.

The sight was marred by a pair of figures in yellow hazmat suits standing out front. As Laughton came up the walk, they turned toward him. One was a man in his midforties with a soft, wide face and a sandy mustache, his thin hair awhirl in his baggy helmet. The other was a lean woman, about the same age, her cheeks shrunken and her lips chapped. They held a butcher-paper banner that said in red paint, "Get thee to a quarantine."

"Chief Laughton," the man said, his voice muffled by his mask. "Haven't seen your wife yet."

"Hi, I'm Aileen," the woman said, holding her hand out to Kir, who shook it.

"Herb. Aileen. What time did you all get out here?" Laughton said.

"Maybe a little before nine," Aileen said.

"Clinic doesn't open until ten," Laughton said. "Why do you keep up this nonsense? You're not going to convince anyone to leave the preserve."

"They need to be reminded," Aileen said. "Especially the

ones who don't remember the plagues," she said, looking at Kir. "You put all these people together, it's like begging for an epidemic. Just one person sick, just one . . ."

"And kids," Herb said, indicating the clinic. "Germ factories. Like a biological nuclear bomb. You want the remaining humans to die out, put them close together where contagion will rage like a wildfire."

"Why'd you two come to the preserve in the first place if you're afraid of another plague?" Kir said.

"Someone's got to warn 'em," Aileen said.

"Just don't pester 'em," Jesse said.

"Mister, I hope you're only visiting," Herb said to Kir. "You don't want to settle here."

"Thanks for the warning," Kir said.

Aileen grabbed Jesse's arm. "You should take that daughter of yours and get somewhere safe, just the three of you," the woman said.

Jesse pulled his arm from her grip. "Just don't be a pest to people," he said again.

He pulled open the door and led the way into the clinic.

If nothing else, Herb and Aileen prepared you for the contrast between the former magnificence of the outside of the clinic to the clinical interior. The floors were cream laminate tiles with streaks of black meant either to imitate marble or just to help disguise any dirt. Walls had been taken down to create a large waiting area where there had most likely once been a sitting room and dining room. Flat-panel TVs graced the walls. A large reception desk stood dead center. The place had already been converted into a medical clinic before the preserve had been established, and it lent itself to its new purpose as solely a fertility clinic. The general medical clinic had since moved into an old office building.

Jamie Cotts sat at the registration desk behind a computer,

a printer, a scanner, and two telephones. She was uncomfortably attractive: dark brown hair, a small slightly upturned nose, large brown eyes that she accentuated with eyeliner and mascara. He wondered how many donors' productions were fueled by fantasies of Jamie.

"Betty's not here yet," Jamie said as Laughton and Kir came up to the desk. The waiting area was empty.

"Herb and Aileen told me," he said.

Jamie shook her head. "I wish they'd go quarantine themselves."

But you don't remember the plagues, Laughton thought, suddenly feeling more charitable to the middle-aged couple.

"Is Moira in?"

"She's in her office. Should I call her?" Jamie said, placing her hand on one of the phone's receivers.

"Can I just go back?" Laughton said.

She looked at Kir.

"He doesn't have to come with me."

She took her hand from the phone. "Sure. There's no one here yet. Slow morning."

Jesse started around the desk, but he then stopped as though he had forgotten something—people tend to give away more when it seems like the question wasn't worth more than an afterthought. He brought out his phone. "Do you recognize either of these men? Maybe donors?"

Jamie looked at the phone. There was no reaction to Sam McCardy, but when he swiped to the photo of Smythe . . .

blink, micro-expression—worry—smile without eyes—withholding

"I can't say. You'll have to ask Moira."

"I'm not just asking as a friend," Laughton said, tapping the badge on his shirt.

The false smile grew. "Ask Moira first."

Anonymity and the sanctity of patient information were the law in the clinic, above the Law with a capital "L," it seemed. "Sure," Laughton said, putting his phone away and giving Kir a look that told his partner to see what he could do. "Buzz me in." He pointed at the door that led to the inner workings of the clinic. It sported a red plastic sign that said, "No Admittance Without An Accompanying Employee." A handwritten sign taped beside it read "Have you registered at a kiosk?"

The door buzzed, disengaging the lock, and the chief pulled hard on the heavy door, stubborn on its pneumatic hinge. The tiles from the waiting area continued in the hall, which Laughton knew formed a square with doors on either side leading to offices, examination rooms, and sperm donor suites. Comfort suites—where couples met—were upstairs. Moira's office was the last door on the left. It was open.

"Knock, knock," Laughton said from the doorway.

"Jesse!" Moira said, standing up from her desk. She had been busy reviewing something on a large computer monitor. She stepped over, and they hugged briefly. "Isn't Betty at school?"

"Yes, I came to see you."

"I'm flattered." Moira was the driving force behind the Liberty Fertility Clinic. She had been active in the repopulation movement for fifteen years, focusing her attention on far-flung humans living outside the cities, often traveling with a portable freezing unit to collect sperm once she had convinced people of the importance of preserving the species and the need for genetic diversity. As part of the movement, she had lobbied for the creation of the preserve and, continuing her good work once the preserve came to be, had opened the clinic in Liberty to assure that those living outside of Charleston were still integral in human development. A passionate woman, Moira was tall with short white hair and remarkably unlined skin. She always wore a white coat and a charm necklace from which five little figures hung, one for each of her children. Betty had met Moira when she was pregnant with Erica, and she looked up to the older woman almost as a mother.

"If you're not here to see Betty, then I think I know why you're here. Ask me what you need to ask me."

Laughton would have liked to sit down, to strike a more relaxed tone, but Moira remained standing. He held out his phone.

"I need to know if either of these men has ever come in here, and who they've seen." Moira took the phone and brought it close to her face to examine. "First is Carl Smythe. Second is Sam McCardy."

Laughton watched the play of the muscles in Moira's face, but they revealed nothing. It seemed likely that she genuinely didn't recognize the men, but hard to say for certain. "I can't release that information without a patient's consent," Moira said.

Laughton took back his phone and pocketed it. "In the case of a murder investigation, you must."

Her eyes grew sharp. "One of these is the man who was killed?"

"Smythe's dead."

"It couldn't last forever," she said.

"Help me minimize the impact. If anyone knew either of the men here, that could make a big difference."

"With a court-ordered subpoena, I'm happy to help," Moira said.

"That's not necessary when it comes to identifying a victim."

"You're not asking me to identify a victim," Moira said.

"Moira, come on," Laughton said. "You're worried about how this case will affect the preserve? Help me out."

Moira's eyebrows pulled together, and the corners of her mouth dipped slightly. "Smythe was here."

So that was another reason he would come to town without a business meeting. "Was he here yesterday?"

Moira smiled. "I can give you name, address, date of birth, but for anything more . . ."

"Moira, you're making me feel like we're not on the same side here."

"If I don't honor my patients' privacy, how am I supposed to get them here?"

"So who he might have seen is out of the question? If he saw anyone."

"Get a subpoena," Moira said. "I'm sorry." She sat down on her desk chair.

Laughton considered sitting down on one of the visitors' chairs to the side of the desk to try to just wait her out, but he didn't think it likely he would be able to change Moira's mind. She hadn't achieved what she'd achieved by being easily swayed. "Can you at least tell me if he participated in the conjugal program or the donor program?"

"Get a subpoena," she repeated. "I want to help you, but you need to get a subpoena."

He didn't think it would be a problem to get one, but it was frustrating and annoying. This felt like the best lead yet, or at least one that was more likely than unraveling the illegal sims trade. That was a loose thread on a sweater; pulling on it would unravel the whole thing. This was a pair of gloves: because it was personal, it would fit. "We both know I'll have the paperwork within the hour. Can't you save me some time?"

She simply smiled.

"I'll be back," he said, and turned to go.

"Make sure the paperwork allows you to access the relevant information of other patients."

Moira also hadn't accomplished what she'd accomplished without being practical.

"Thank you," Laughton said. "At least I know I won't be wasting my time."

"See you soon."

"Soon," Laughton said. He went back down the hall and hit the release button on the wall to disengage the magnetic lock. In the waiting area, Kir was leaning on the desk with a wry smile, saying something to Jamie. They both looked at Jesse as he rounded the desk.

"Your partner—"

"Ex-partner," Laughton said.

"Was just telling me about when Erica was born, that you and Betty had wanted a human midwife, but there were none available."

"Listen, Jamie," he said, trying to strike a casual tone, "Moira said Smythe came in, but she couldn't remember if he saw only one person or if it was a few."

Before Jamie could even register the question, the word "Liberty" from the television caught the attention of all three of them. It was one of the few preserve channels that broadcast out of Charleston, news anchor Kara Letts. The closed captions that were popping up one word at a time in little black bars said, "Again, a body was found behind the Kramer's Supermarket in Liberty late yesterday. The Charleston Police and the HHS had a joint press conference this morning . . ."

The phone in Laughton's pocket buzzed, two quick pulses that meant he'd received a text message. That would be the commissioner, no doubt.

Jamie looked at him. "Is it true?" she said.

He nodded once. "It's true."

She shook her head without even realizing she was doing it. "That's why you're here," she said to Kir.

"It is," he said.

Laughton felt guilty trying to take advantage of her distress, but he was now in even more of a rush. He repeated, "Moira said Smythe came in, but she couldn't remember who he saw."

Jamie's mouth went sideways and her eyes narrowed, replacing her concern with caution. "Why do I think I still shouldn't tell you?"

It had been worth a try. "No problem," he said, making it sound like it really was no problem. "Have Betty call me when she gets in."

He had his phone out as he went through the front door, and was surprised to find the text was from Dunrich. It said "Call now." Dunrich would have to wait a minute. Laughton needed to get his damn subpoena first.

The phone buzzed in his hand. Mathews. "Laughton," he said, answering it.

"Are the tech guys supposed to be human?" Mathews said.

"I would think so," he said.

"What is it?" Kir said.

"Because a car pulled up across the street. Two guys in it, but they're not getting out, so I tried a facial scan from here for the one that's closer, and it's a bad angle and at a distance, but, files say robot."

"That doesn't mean shit with a crappy angle."

"Why are they just sitting in the car?"

Laughton didn't even want to consider how there could be robots on the house. "Sit tight," he said. "Wait for the real techs, and keep an eye on the guys in the car."

"And if they try to come in?"

"Alert me if they even move."

"Okay, Chief," Mathews said, but it didn't sound like it was okay.

"Hang tight," Laughton said. "And send me a visual."

Mathews hung up.

"What is it?" Kir said.

The phone buzzed, and Laughton opened up the photo. "These guys mean anything to you?" He held out the phone to Kir.

"Where is this?" Kir said.

"Outside Sam and Smythe's place."

"Those are off-the-shelf faces," Kir said.

Robots. "Shit."

"Titanium has a few working for him, but it's impossible to know if these are the ones."

"They're on the preserve, it doesn't matter who they work for."

"I forwarded it to the secretary," Kir said. "She'll tell me what she wants to do."

"What the fuck, Kir? You don't ask me first?"

"Like you told Jamie," Kir said, "we're *ex*-partners."

"So you're 'the man' now?" he said.

"I'm 'the man,'" the robot answered with no hint of a smile.

"Because, if we're working together, I need to know you're not broadcasting everything. Otherwise, you can get off now."

Kir was silent, his robot face impassive in a way that was inhuman. "You're right. It won't happen again."

"How do I know?"

"Because I'm telling you."

Laughton tried to fight the feeling Kir would be sending everything back to Pattermann, and to remember who he was dealing with. He thought back to Erica's birth. Kir had come to the hospital, and had been the first to hold Erica other than Betty, Jesse, and the medical staff. The expression on Kir's face had been completely human—if he had been able to cry, he would have. The memory made Jesse's eyes sting. "All right," he said. "And if there is shit that's 'need to know,' I need to know."

"Jesse, if you need to know, I'll tell you. I promise."

"Fuck you," he said. "You better."

They were at the car. As they got back underway, Laughton said, "Who's Titanium? You said someone named Titanium has robots like the ones at Sam and Smythe's."

"Sims distributor."

"Sam and Smythe used someone called the Sisters."

"Titanium is new to the preserve. I'd hoped your case would end up being part of that turf war, but when you said Smythe wrote a burning program . . . Now if they're here, I don't know. Any luck in there?"

"Director of the clinic wants a subpoena before she'll reveal anything." He took out his phone. "I'll email the district attorney now. Maybe we'll still get lucky."

"Maybe."

As it was the first murder on the preserve, and the first suspicious death in his jurisdiction, Chief Laughton had no idea where the coroner's office was. The Medical University of South Carolina was the only major hospital on the preserve, but it was a confusion of buildings spread over several blocks, some linked by walkways that bridged the city streets, others isolated, cut off from the rest of the medical campus by houses and food establishments and phone stores. The sheer number of people was disorienting. Laughton had become used to Liberty's sparse population. Here there were nurses in scrubs carrying takeout, doctors in white coats chatting on benches, wheelchair-bound patients with their bags piled on their laps waiting for rides.

The car navigated to the front entrance, bringing them to a triangular drop-off loop with painted yellow curbs. He shut off the car.

"This is a No Parking zone," Kir said.

Laughton opened his door. "We're the police," he said, and got out, just as his phone started buzzing. He stopped to check it, feeling the air-conditioned air wash over him as the hospital's automatic glass doors slid open for someone else. A photo of Betty and Erica, cheek to cheek, showed on his phone. Erica was laughing, not looking at the camera; Betty had clearly tickled her to get her to smile. He answered it. "Hey."

"My mom fell," Betty said. Betty's mother was in her mid-seventies. She lived in a house around the corner from the Laughtons.

"Is she okay?"

"She hit her face on something. She has some broken teeth, and I don't know what else. Mom, no, don't try to talk."

"She's with you?"

"We're on our way to Charleston. About half an hour out."

"I'm just getting to the hospital now," Laughton said.

"Well, you're going to have to get back to Liberty and pick up Erica at aftercare."

"Okay."

"She can be there until six."

"Okay."

"I don't know how long we'll be once we get to the hospital, so you need to get back there."

"Get Erica by six. Got it." Uncle Kir could surprise her with Laughton.

"How's your day going?" she asked, but Laughton knew she didn't really want to know. Her mind was in emergency mode.

"Fine," he said. "Let me know if you need me."

"Okay." Her tone changed to frustration. "Damn."

"It'll be okay," he said.

"Mom, it's fine," Betty said to her mother. "Don't talk!"

"You go," Laughton said. "I'm busy here. Keep me posted."

"I love you," she said, and hung up.

The chief felt so far away that that didn't even land on him.

"What now?" Kir said.

"Betty's mom fell and needs to come here, so we need to get back to Liberty to pick up Erica by six."

"When it rains . . ."

Laughton pocketed his phone. "Let's find this guy."

There was a security guard just inside the door. The chief

asked him for directions, and he smiled and nodded, pointing out the front desk. "Don't forget your masks," the guard said.

Laughton rolled his eyes. Wearing surgical face masks was his least favorite part of being in a hospital. He hated the warm, damp feeling of his own breath coating his cheeks and nose, but it was the law. He took one from the dispenser, and fit the elastics over his ears. "You better take one too," Laughton said to Kir. "You'll call attention to yourself if you're not wearing one."

Kir smiled, amused by the novelty of wearing the mask. "Human?" he said when his was in place.

"Sure," Laughton said. "Come on."

A heavyset, middle-aged woman with an extravagant glass necklace and matching earrings stood as they approached the desk. The wrinkles around her eyes gave away the smile hidden beneath her own mask. Everyone was very cheerful here, it seemed.

He showed her his badge. "I'm looking for the medical examiner."

Her face scrunched up. "I don't know who that is," she said, reaching for a phone on her desk. "Give me one moment." She dialed, waited a few seconds, and then asked someone named Terry if she knew who the medical examiner was. Terry must have asked some people on her end, because it was at least a minute before the woman in front of him hung up, and said, "Let me just try someone else." She dialed and put the phone to her ear again, waiting.

Great, Laughton thought. Maybe he should have just waited for the ME's report. It'd be sent to him in the morning. For all he knew, he'd missed the autopsy.

The woman hung up, and said, "I'm so sorry. No one seems to know who that is. Is there anyone you could ask on your end?"

Laughton looked at Kir.

Kir shrugged. "Can you tell us where the morgue is?"

She looked at the screen in front of her, typed something on a keyboard, swiped the screen, and then pointed toward a bank of elevators. "Take those elevators there down to the basement," she said, and gave intricate directions that Laughton didn't bother to remember, knowing Kir recorded them automatically.

A pair of doctors in long white coats exited the elevator when it came. It wasn't until the doors closed and he'd pushed the button for the basement that Laughton registered that one of them had not been wearing a mask—a Dr. Check model, the ubiquitous medical robot he'd seen all his life. Perhaps he was naive, but he'd really thought there were actually no robots on the preserve. He guessed some medical procedures must be best left to a robot, which explained why one would be in the hospital. Still, if he'd thought it was jarring to see so many people, it was even more shocking to see a robot. He'd never have believed there'd ever be such a time in his life, but it had actually been months since he had seen a robot. With his record broken, he realized how much he had liked it.

He started to say something about it to Kir, and then it struck him that Kir was a robot. His streak had already been broken that morning, he just didn't think of Kir in those terms.

The basement was like a tunnel, with bundles of pipes and wires hanging overhead. The lighting was naked bulbs, and there were painted metal doors along the way with scuffs and dents. They reached another elevator, and Kir stopped, pushing the call button.

"We have to go back upstairs?" Laughton said.

"There's actually another floor below us," Kir said.

This elevator was an oversize freight elevator, large enough to hold three gurneys at once. Empty, it felt like a room.

Downstairs, the hallway seemed narrow, a result of the sanitize chamber that had been retrofitted along the outside of the morgue in the aftermath of the first pandemic. Inside the chamber there were benches and spare hazmat suits. It was cold, colder than the rest of the hospital. Through the window of the inner door, Laughton could see eight cadavers laid out on stainless steel tables and covered with sheets. Three medical students in hazmat suits were gathered around one of the tables, their corpse uncovered, its chest open. One of them was hunched over the body, her hands in the cavity as she made careful cuts to remove one of the organs. A tablet on a stand showed a painting of some anatomical structure.

Sitting on a stool at a high shelf was an older man with thick gray hair, not wearing a suit or even a mask. *If he doesn't have to wear one*, Laughton thought, *then no way I am.* The chief pressed the release button to the side of the inner door. A red light flashed, and with a thunk, the outer door locked, and the light turned green as the lock disengaged on the inner door.

The smell in the room was like a physical assault, a burning in the back of the throat. It mixed with Chief Laughton's headache to send a wave of nausea from his gut to his mouth. Where did they get this many human bodies?

The older man had stood when Laughton and Kir walked in. Now, as they approached, he said, "May I help you?"

Laughton showed him his ID, taking off his own mask. "You are . . . ?"

"Dr. Conroy," the older man said. Then the ID registered. "You're working the murder?"

"Yes."

"That's why *he's* here," Dr. Conroy said. Then to Kir, "Why are you bothering to wear that?" he said.

Kir said, "Jesse thought it would help me blend in." He left it on. "I kind of like it."

Dr. Conroy shrugged. "I was just finishing up the report," he said, gesturing to the tablet sitting on his high desk.

"The autopsy's done?"

"I didn't get any word that someone was coming."

"Nobody knew who to contact," Jesse said.

"They knew where to send the body."

"Bodies go to morgues," Kir said.

Dr. Conroy said, "Well, you want to look?" He stepped around Chief Laughton, and led them the length of the room. Built-in cabinets and a counter ran down the back wall. Fluorescent lights under the cabinets lit the various bottles and supply bins neatly organized on the counter. A large bank of stainless steel sinks was along the short wall. A light array hung on an articulated arm above each table. Dr. Conroy took them to the farthest table. He pulled the sheet off of the body, bunching it up in his arms.

Carl Smythe, his torso sporting the traditional Y-shaped incision, stitched up now, was laid out on the table. The simulskin on the arm and leg had been peeled off, leaving just the metal skeleton. Seeing the metal alongside the organic body was disorienting. It reminded Laughton of photographs he had seen as a child of fantastical creatures that showmen of the nineteenth and twentieth centuries used to make by gluing parts of different animals together, claiming they had mermaids or missing links on display. He had no problem with cyborgs. He knew some like Smythe had no choice.

Dr. Conroy tilted Smythe's head to the side with gloved hands, and raised the shoulder in order to better reveal the Taser wound. The area around the two puncture points was red and slightly shiny. The punctures themselves had been cleaned, any encrusted blood washed away, but they still appeared darker than Laughton would have expected. "The subject was Tasered at close range," Conroy said. "The puncture points are singed, which suggests to me the Taser might even have been pressed up against his neck when it was fired. The burns aren't so bad to suggest that the Taser was left in place for a long time, though, and without a continued or repeated charge, a Taser shouldn't have killed him. But the wounds are right on the wiring for his prosthetics, in fact with almost impossible precision. High enough charge overloaded the system, instant heart attack. Like ancient electric chairs."

"Go back. You said 'impossible precision.' Why 'impossible'?"

"Because the wiring can't be located from outside, and it's not like the victim would have stood still while his killer looked for it, anyway. To have caught it so perfectly is either luck or—"

"Someone with X-ray vision," Kir said. "Meaning, a robot."

Conroy shrugged. "Possibly."

"Any signs of struggle? Fingernails? Scrapes?"

"No. If you ask me, I'd say the murderer came up behind the victim, grabbed him and Tasered him before the victim even knew someone was there."

"And what's with the arm and leg?"

"I'd say childhood accident," Conroy said. He pointed out the spot where the metal met the flesh. "The electronic ports are old, maybe fifteen, twenty years. The limbs are newer. Means they've been replaced at least once. If they were from childhood, probably more than once. They're a basic model, though. Nothing special."

"So why were they cut up?"

Conroy went over to a sink and counter in the corner and came back with an oversize Ziploc bag that contained the mess of simul-skin he had removed from the corpse. He pulled a piece out. Simul-skin didn't hold fingerprints well. They'd no doubt been dusted already. He unraveled the skin and pointed out what looked like a little pocket on the underside of the forearm. "My guess is that they were looking for something."

"Was it there? Did they get it?"

"Well, we didn't get it, so I'm guessing they did. Couldn't have been bigger than a finger, probably a memory stick."

"He hid it in his body?" Laughton's face clenched in disgust.

Conroy shrugged. He was indifferent to the practice. He returned the simul-skin to the evidence bag, and tossed it back on the counter.

Laughton looked at Kir. "Thoughts?"

"Yes," Kir said without elaborating.

"We have no way of knowing anything was actually in the arm," Laughton said, although it seemed likely.

"No," Conroy said.

Laughton closed his eyes for a moment to think. He shook his head. So if something was hidden in the arm, that could have been the motive. What was it? He opened his eyes. "Okay," he said. "Thanks."

"I'll have the report tonight, but I told you everything that matters."

"Thanks," Laughton said again.

"I know it's not much." The doctor seemed almost embarrassed in his apology, like he'd failed by not finding more.

"Nice meeting you," Laughton said. "Don't take this the wrong way, but, I hope I never have to see you again."

Conroy looked at Kir. "And I hope I never see you again."

"So do I," Kir said. "Tell me, why don't you wear the suit? Isn't it required?"

Dr. Conroy said, "The suits just make people feel better.

If another plague is coming, it won't be a suit and a couple of doors that save me."

Laughton replaced his mask, though, just so he wouldn't get a hard time from security. "In the long run," he said, "nothing can save you."

"You don't have to tell me," the doctor said as they filed past the filled tables, back to the air-lock door.

———

"So what do you think Smythe had stashed away in that little pocket?" Laughton asked as they waited for the elevator.

"Memory stick seems like a good guess to me," Kir said.

"But if Smythe *is* the source of the killer app, why would he be hiding it after it's already in the wild?"

The elevator came, and they got on. "Unless it's a nonexecutable copy, one that let him work on it. If people figured out a way to neutralize it, he'd want a copy to tweak."

Laughton nodded. "Or it's the antivirus."

"If he wanted to kill robots, why bother with an antivirus?"

The elevator opened, and they moved down the hall toward the other elevator. "Maybe it was the first step in a ransom scheme. Let a few robots die, then come forward with the antivirus with a huge price tag."

"I don't know," Kir said. "Most robots would think the addicts using sims deserved what they got. The government's not going to be able to put money toward that."

"But the sims dealers might. They don't want all of their customers getting fried."

Kir tilted his head. "That might work."

"It'd be a reason to kill Smythe, to get the antivirus."

"Or even the source code."

"Could be worth a lot of money."

The elevator opened at the lobby. They stepped out, giving way for others to get on. Jesse stopped short. "We should see if Betty and her mom are here before we leave." He turned. "Excuse me, can you hold—?"

A young man holding a child propped in the crux of one arm put his hand out, and the elevator door stopped closing and reopened.

"Thank you," Laughton said as they stepped on. The ER was marked on the elevator panel as one floor below them. Laughton smiled at the little boy in his father's arms, and then remembered that the boy couldn't see his mouth behind the mask. The mask covering the boy's mouth covered almost his entire face and hung below his chin. They must have been out of child-size masks.

When the door slid open, Laughton said, "Take care," and he and Kir stepped out. There was the subdued, waiting room hush of a lot of people attempting to make very little noise. There were two televisions, just loud enough to create a murmur, but not loud enough to be understood. Jesse started to scan the people in the chairs, when Kir grabbed his arm, and pulled him around.

"Who would have known Smythe had the virus or antivirus on him?"

Jesse felt his whole jaw tighten, the muscles below his left eye tingling. "Sam McCardy, who I stupidly let get away."

"Or his middleman, Jones."

"Who I also let get away."

"Don't beat yourself up. You can't just hold people for no reason."

"Says the robot police officer."

"I never held anyone if it broke the law," Kir said, his voice harsh.

"I know," Laughton said, shaking his head. "I know. I didn't mean anything. I just feel like an idiot."

"Well, don't. Letting Jones go makes sense. We'll track him down later."

"But not leaving someone to watch McCardy was lazy," Laughton said.

"We can't all be me," Kir said.

"Fuck you."

"Hey, it might be one of the women Smythe was seeing at the clinic, and then it's a moot point," Kir said.

Laughton thought that was unlikely, but Kir was right that it couldn't be ruled out. "Okay," he said.

"Don't feel stupid," Kir said. "We're on this thing."

"Tell it to your boss."

"I have."

"Jesse?"

Betty was walking toward them. Her pace increased as she approached, and she threw her arms around his waist. He pulled her in tight as she sighed into him. "You okay?" he said.

She nodded against his shoulder. "Just exhausted."

"Tell me about it."

Betty stepped back, and then she hugged Kir as well. "It's good to see you," she said.

Laughton saw his mother-in-law in one of the seats nearest to the TV. He went over to her. "Barbara, how are you?"

She wasn't wearing a mask. Her lips were swollen to twice their usual size with a dried, red cut in the center of the lower lip. Her nose looked out of place with more blood crusted around one nostril, and a bruise trailing across her cheekbone. She just shook her head, and blinked.

"Hurts too much to talk?" he said.

She nodded.

"What happened?"

She shook her head again.

Betty and Kir had joined them, Betty taking the seat next to her mother. "Mom, this is Jesse's old partner, Kir."

The old woman nodded that she recognized him.

"He's here because of the murder."

"What happened?" Jesse said to Betty.

"I don't know," Betty said. "She went upstairs for something, and when she came back down, she fell."

"They tell you how long until it's your turn?"

"No." There were at least thirty other people waiting. "What'd you find?"

"You know I can't discuss it," Laughton said.

"Because *I'm* a danger!" Betty said.

He raised his eyebrows and gestured at the rest of the room, indicating all of the other people.

"Oh, right," she said.

"Betty, we've got this," Kir said.

"He keeps saying that," Jesse said.

"Because it's true."

"Well, don't forget to pick up Erica by six if you don't hear from me," Betty said.

"I won't," Laughton said.

"I won't let him," Kir said.

"Okay."

"Keep me posted," Laughton said, and he bent down to kiss her through his mask. To his mother-in-law, he said, "I'd kiss you, but I'm afraid to hurt you."

She nodded her understanding.

Laughton heard a familiar voice, and he looked over to the television. They were re-airing the press conference from earlier in the day with the commissioner, the secretary of Health and Human Services, and Brandis. It made his stomach turn. "I don't want to see this shit again," he said to Kir, and headed for the elevator without waiting for his partner.

His phone buzzed as he and Kir stepped into the elevator. He pulled it out. "Yes," he said, looking at the screen. "Subpoena's in." He hit forward, and sent it to Moira. "Let's get back to Liberty; try to interview at least one of the women this afternoon."

"We need to make a stop first," Kir said.

They were back in the main lobby. "Police headquarters. Secretary Pattermann wants to see us while we're in town."

"Shit," Laughton said, pulling off his mask as they exited the hospital. "I should probably see the commissioner."

"The secretary promised it won't be long."

"She better not be. Our job is policing, not politics," Jesse said.

"Most of the time," Kir said, "it's the same thing."

———

The Charleston Police Department's headquarters was across the street from a small riverside park. Metal posts placed at equal distances lined a paved walk. The grass was well tended, the few trees wearing young leaves. Across the water, rows of small, probably no longer owned yachts were anchored along a pier, sun bleached, algaed, and barnacled, but from this side of the river, white and grand, and suggestive of freedom and money. Beyond that, a gray skyline described the city of the distant shore. If you were in lockup and lucky enough to be on the right side of the building, the view must have made the stay more bearable. It was probably prisoners who did the park's grounds keeping, after all.

The headquarters looked like the kind of high school they

had built eighty or ninety years ago, red brick stained black with grime, opaque green glass windows, concrete steps, and a later addition tacked on to the side, a tan brick building with a grid of small square windows. For a minute, Chief Laughton stood with the park on his left and headquarters on his right, looking from one to the other. The river was the promise of the preserve, the headquarters its reality.

"How come we only got a view of the highway from head-quarters in Baltimore?" Laughton said to Kir.

"We were only five minutes from the water."

"And how often did we walk over to the water? Oh, never."

"It's not my fault you were unimaginative."

"How about we just go sit on a bench for a little while?"

"You do that," Kir said.

Then Jesse's phone buzzed. "And the phone again." He pulled it out.

There was an older message that he must have missed at some point. Mathews letting him know that the tech people had arrived at the hackers' house, and that the robots had taken off when they saw the other cops show up.

The new notification was an email from Moira with Smythe's clinical record. The hacker had seen three women over the past nine months. Two only once each right when the clinic opened, and then a woman named Nancy Enright, once a week for the last few months. He wondered how Miss Enright was handling Carl's death. He held the phone out so Kir could see. "Smythe had a lover," he said.

"Good to hear."

"Let's go," Laughton said. "I don't want to waste any more time here than I have to."

Inside, headquarters had a similar vibe to the hospital, large and impersonal. Many people were on their way out, the day over for them. The commissioner sent a uniform down to escort Laughton and Kir to his office. The nametag pinned on the uniform's shirt read "A. Knightly." He was maybe twenty years old, clean-shaven, and sported close-cropped hair. He walked with his eyes straight ahead in such a way that Laughton knew he was using all his willpower to not look in the chief's or Kir's direction. Was it Kir that was making the boy so nervous?

When they reached the commissioner's office, Laughton said, "Thank you."

Officer Knightly met his eyes. "You're welcome. Anything you need."

Laughton saw what he had taken to be nerves was actually admiration. He couldn't understand why.

The commissioner was sitting at his desk with his eyes closed. There was a flutter in his lower lip that belied the appearance of calm. But it was the woman sitting in the chair in front of the commissioner's desk that commanded Laughton's attention. Grace Pattermann. Laughton had seen her on the news countless times. Seeing her in person was unreal. Small and compact as she was, she seemed bigger than anyone else in the room.

"Gentlemen," she said by way of greeting.

The commissioner took three deep breaths, then opened his eyes. "Five minutes of regular breathing and I feel refreshed."

"Good for you." Laughton genuinely meant the comment, but he could see the commissioner took it as sarcasm.

"You should try it," he said.

Maybe I should, Laughton thought.

"Madam Secretary," Kir said.

She held up her hand. "I know you both know what's at stake here today," the secretary said. "But I want you to understand how dire the situation actually is. Brandis has asked the president to bring army forces onto the preserve."

"That's ridiculous," Laughton said.

Secretary's lower eyelids tense, lips tighten—mild anger

Kir put a silencing hand on Laughton's shoulder.

"It is ridiculous, Chief Laughton. A single murder is not civil unrest, but Brandis is trying to blow this murder out of proportion. He can't decide if he should claim it's part of a sims war or if it's just evidence of humans' natural violence."

"What's the president said?" Kir said.

"He's using caution, but if more robots die from this bad sim and it really did come from the preserve, then he won't be able to be cautious much longer."

"So, first," the commissioner said. "Is it?"

"Is it what?" Laughton said.

"Is it tied to this bad sim, killer app, whatever?"

Laughton looked from one to the other. Would it be better to equivocate? It was all speculation right now. Just because the victim *could* have been the creator of the killer app didn't mean he *was*. They had no evidence one way or the other. "What's better?" he said to Secretary Pattermann. "Forewarned or plausible deniability?"

"Deniability is always an option," the secretary said, "regardless of what was actually known. That's why it's denial, and not definitive."

"Then," Chief Laughton said, "I think probably, yes, but . . ."

"Shit," the commissioner said.

"No, I needed to know that," the secretary said. "It will make it more difficult, but at least I can plan for it."

"Plan to have robots swarming all over the place," the commissioner said. "I can barely keep the feds off us about the sims coming out of the preserve, as if there was really any way to control it and I don't have a million other things to worry about."

"A murder was going to be a lightning rod no matter the circumstances," Secretary Pattermann said.

"Not if it was a simple domestic, and we had the man in jail within the hour."

Laughton felt that as a slam against him, the muscles in his shoulders seizing and his cheek throbbing.

"This does make it harder," the secretary said.

"So where are we on this?" the commissioner said. "What did the ME say?"

"Taser hit the wiring for Smythe's arm at close range with precision," Kir answered.

"Does that mean anything?"

"No. Not really."

"So, do you have anything else?"

"Your tech people are at the hackers' house, right?" Laughton said.

The commissioner nodded. "They're supposed to report to you when they find anything."

"We've got another lead too," Kir said. "A mistress."

"That would be better," the secretary said.

"Who are we kidding?" the commissioner said.

"We're keeping track of their distributor," Laughton said, stretching the truth a little about Jones. "I've got people tracking down other hackers, trying to find if anyone knew these people. They were like fucking hermits. And the vic has a sister who lives off-preserve. We're tracking her too."

"So we've got nothing," the commissioner said.

"Not nothing," the secretary said.

"That's optimistic," the commissioner said.

"That's half of my job," Secretary Pattermann said. She turned her attention to Laughton and Kir. The force of her eyes through the red rims of her glasses inspired the conviction to deliver. "We do not have much time on this," she said.

"Then let us go do our job," Kir said.

"For as long as I can," the secretary said.

The commissioner laced his hands together and ran them over the top of his head, causing the hair to stick up. "The FBI wants in on this case," he said. "If the sims connection is correct, there's nothing we're going to be able to do to stop them."

"And the Coast Guard," the secretary said. "Since they police the harbor, they feel they have a say."

"Anyone else?" Laughton said.

"We knew there would be a murder," the secretary said. "People kill each other. That happens. But this sims connection . . ."

Laughton was so beat down that part of him felt like it would be a blessing to let the metals come in and take over, but he thought of Erica growing up in a robot-free environment, where she wouldn't have to face arrogant metals treating them like animals or worry about hate crimes that the robot world just ignored . . . The idea that that all rested on him was staggering.

"What more do you need?" the secretary said.

Laughton shook his head. "I don't know." He thought of all those books. "They used old paper books. Maybe they had a bookseller."

"Yeah. The internet," the commissioner said.

"Something else to look out for," Laughton said.

"I'm going to keep stalling," the secretary said. "That's my job, that's my life, stall, stall, stall. But we need this tied up, gentlemen."

"Buy us the time," Kir said. "Keep us informed. We'll tie it up."

"Never-ending energy, never-ending optimism," Laughton said. Something flashed on the commissioner's face.

narrowing on the outside edges of the eyes, slight downturn of the corner of upper lip—worry

"What is it?" Laughton said.

"Nothing," the commissioner said.

Secretary Pattermann said, "It's good to see you in person, Chief Laughton. Kir speaks of you often. I have utter faith in you both. Just don't put too much faith in me."

"Yes, ma'am," Laughton said.

Kir gave his boss a respectful nod.

The commissioner had closed his eyes again and slowed his breathing.

If only, Laughton thought. *If only what?*

"Get going," Secretary Pattermann said.

Nancy Enright lived in a twenty-first-century home about a mile and a half outside of Liberty's downtown. An oversize box, the main impression it made was as an expanse of vinyl siding, remarkably clean. There was no ornamentation, no shrubbery, no porch or shutters; the point had been big, even at the expense of being bland. At one time, it had no doubt replaced an older, smaller home, encroaching on Liberty's nineteenth-century roots, but *it* was the anachronism now, the rest of the block occupied by townhomes with plate glass fronts. Those had all been overtaken by vegetation, ivy and tufts of Spanish moss, piles of windswept, dry leaves beside each home's stairs, no longer fresh or hip. Laughton wondered how the Enright home had survived redevelopment and then survived abandonment. Perhaps it had retained human residents through the years. Maybe the Enrights had always lived there, even before the preserve.

Laughton and Kir left the car in the empty driveway, and peeked through the garage windows for no particular reason outside of occupational nosiness. There were at least five bicycles ranging in size from a beginner bike to adult, the children's bikes lying willy-nilly on top of one another. The rest of the space was given over to cardboard boxes and plastic totes. No car could fit in there.

"Big family," Kir said.

"Let's hope someone's home."

When they reached the front door, a blue LED light

flashed on a small camera mounted at eye level. Laughton switched his own body cam on, looked square into the house security camera's lens, and waited for the door to open. He heard a child shout, "I'll get it," while another shrieked, the sound coming closer, but before either could respond, the door was opened by a petite Asian woman. She had straight black hair pulled into a loose ponytail draped over one shoulder. Her blue-and-white sweaterdress revealed the subtle bump of early pregnancy. The smaller of the two children Laughton had heard elected to hide behind his mother, and the woman held the older one close, her arm over his shoulder, hand on his chest. A third child appeared in the entryway behind her, and then ran off. The children's eyes were not as narrow as their mother's. Their father must have not been of Asian descent.

"Miss Enright?" Laughton said, displaying his badge.

lower eyelid droop, corner of lips flick down for a fraction of a second, then neutral—concealed sadness

"Come in," she said, resigned.

Laughton stepped into the house, his partner behind him. It smelled of some kind of artificial citrus cleaner. He noticed that several of the floor tiles in the foyer were cracked. Miss Enright led them up a half flight of stairs into the kitchen, which had a vaulted ceiling and glass windows that revealed a small backyard. There was a baby in a high chair wearing a bib with green mush forming a clown's smile around her mouth. Miss Enright sat down at a chair facing the baby, and picked up a plastic spoon. The older of the children who had come to the door decided that the detectives weren't about to be interesting, and he ran down another set of stairs, yelling a battle cry. The toddler stood with one hand on his mother's lap, and watched Laughton with large, distrustful eyes as the chief of police took another of the seats at the table. Kir walked around the table, looking out a window into the backyard.

"It's about Carl," Miss Enright said, keeping her eyes on the baby as she offered her another dollop of green on the spoon.

"Yes," Laughton said.

"I didn't know him well," she said. Her manner was regretful more than sad. "I certainly have no idea who might have hurt him."

Hurt, not kill. "You met him at the Liberty Fertility Clinic?" Laughton said.

"Yes," she said, still feeding the baby.

"How'd that work?" Kir said, still standing, looking out the window.

Nancy glanced at the robot, and resettled her weight in the chair with a slight rock back and forth. "You fill out a form, and they pair you up. As long as there's some attraction, you . . . mate."

"Do you see a lot of men at the clinic?" Laughton said.

"I've seen others, but not in a long time, not since Carl and I met."

"Why Carl?" Kir said.

Laughton realized that he and Kir had fallen into their old routine, alternating questions, keeping the interviewee off balance. It felt good.

"He just had energy," Miss Enright said, still talking to the baby instead of settling on either of the policemen; preventing Laughton from seeing her face. "Just everything about him, the fast way he talked, and the exuberance with which he moved. It was apparent before you even said hello to him. He brought that enthusiasm to bed."

"Why didn't you come forward when you heard he'd died?" Laughton said.

"I didn't think I knew anything helpful, and my husband doesn't know that I do conjugal visits at the clinic. He can get jealous."

"Most men would."

"I'm committed to repopulation, and part of the success of the project is a diverse genetic makeup. That means more than having babies just the two of us."

"So, if your husband wanted to go to the clinic?" Kir said.

She bit the inside of her lower lip, and nodded. "I'd allow it."

Laughton pointed at the children with his chin. "Any of these children Carl's?"

"I've known Carl maybe seven months," she said.

Right, stupid question, Laughton thought. "Is the one you're carrying Carl's?"

She shrugged as though it really didn't matter. "Maybe."

"Would your husband have a reason to think the baby wasn't his? You said he could get jealous," Kir said.

"My husband and I still have plenty of sex, if that's what you're asking."

"I guess that sort of is what we were asking," Laughton said.

She looked from Laughton to Kir, but then quickly away from the robot, raising her shoulders defensively. Kir was making her nervous. "Look, Bobby doesn't know about the conjugal visits," she said, addressing Laughton in particular. "He certainly doesn't know I had a regular partner, and besides, Bobby couldn't hurt anybody."

Of course, that's what people always believed, Laughton thought. He looked at Kir, who was watching him, waiting for a signal. The robot knew Miss Enright was emotional, but wasn't quite certain what the emotion was. Laughton tugged at the front of his shirt to convey that she was angry, a stylized gesture that had its origin in American Sign Language, but mutated into something that could seem natural. Kir, however, interpreted Laughton's cue as a sign to push harder, instead of changing the subject, which is what Laughton wanted.

"Where is your husband now?" Kir said.

Her flash of anger had her near tears of sadness now. She appealed to Laughton with her eyes. "It wasn't Bobby."

"Okay," Laughton said, holding up his hands in a placating gesture. "Okay. We just need to check all possibilities."

She looked back at the baby, who hit the spoon out of her hand. "Are you all finished? Are you all finished?" She picked up a cloth from the table, and wiped off the baby's face.

"Can you tell us anything?" Laughton said. "Anything he might have said, any calls he might have made in front of you, anything could be helpful, even if it doesn't seem like it would be."

She shook her head as she stood to take the baby out of the high chair. "No. Nothing. I've been trying to think."

Laughton didn't say anything, and Kir knew not to either. Sometimes keeping silent was the easiest way to get someone to talk. It forced her to fill up the silence.

"He'd get texts all of the time, but he said it was some game he played online."

Laughton wondered if they'd located Smythe's phone yet.

She put the baby down on the floor and the child just sat. The toddler squatted so that his face was an inch away from his sister's. She grabbed her brother's nose. Miss Enright sat back down, and looked at Laughton. "We'd talk sometimes. Just about nothing. I think we both tried to keep our personal lives secret, but it becomes hard when you see someone once or twice a week."

"See" them, Laughton thought.

Miss Enright's eyes tilted to the side and went out of focus.

She was trying to recall anything, making a real effort. "He talked about robots a lot. He called them M-E-T-A-L-S," she spelled for the benefit of the children. "I think he hated them, really hated them." She checked to see how that information was landing on Kir, but the robot's face was impassive, impossible to read.

"What'd he say?" Laughton said to draw her attention back to him. The tag team hadn't been working—she was too disconcerted by Kir's presence—so the robot had let Laughton have full control.

She shook her head. "I don't know." Her eyes darted to Kir again.

Just then there was some kind of crash in the living room downstairs. "Is everything all right!" Miss Enright called.

"Yes!" a child replied.

"I'll go check," Kir said, heading down the stairs before Miss Enright could react.

Laughton saw the tension at her temples. She didn't like the idea of Kir alone with any of her kids. Laughton wondered if that had been Kir's intention, or if his partner had just thought that getting out of the room would free up the conversation. Or maybe both.

Laughton tried to draw her back in. "You were saying Carl hated robots . . ."

Her head was cocked, listening for any sound coming from the living room.

"Miss Enright?"

She blinked, and shook her head. "Um, stuff about how they're not really alive, that they're like a, I don't know, a toaster or something, just something that's supposed to be a tool, and who are they to push around their masters, stuff like that." Her eyes darted to the stairs by which Kir had left the kitchen.

"Did you agree?"

"I don't know." She noticed that the toddler at her feet was patting the baby on the head, and the baby was not happy. She tapped the back of the toddler's hand. "Stop that." Then back to Laughton, "I try not to think like that, hate. We know what we did because of hate, humans. I'd just let Carl rant if he needed to. He was lonely."

"You think he might have gotten jealous of your husband? Maybe went to talk to him?"

"No." She shook her head, certain. "Carl saw what we were doing as a way to strike at the robots. He was committed to the cause. I knew he lived way out in the middle of nowhere, and I don't think he was looking to change that."

So Carl had believed in the Liberty Fertility Center's mission. He hadn't just been looking to get laid.

Miss Enright leaned forward. "Is he all right in there? Do I have to worry?"

Laughton followed her gaze to the doorway, then looked back at her worry. "He's fine."

"I just thought . . . How come he's here?"

She meant, how was there a robot on the preserve? "Carl's death is a big deal."

She sat back, but her eyes didn't leave the doorway, as though she could will everything to be all right from her seat.

"Did you know Carl was a cyborg?" Laughton said.

Miss Enright sat up straight in her chair in genuine surprise, her cheeks flushed, distracted from her vigilance. She hadn't known. "No. Which . . . ?" It wasn't a polite question.

"An arm and a leg," Laughton answered.

Her eyes went out of focus. She was remembering, trying to think if she had missed any indication.

"Is that a problem?"

"I . . . No, no," she said; she wasn't a bigot. "That must—Carl would always say they'd taken too much from him. I thought he just meant the way they've taken from all of us, that we're stuffed on the preserve here, but maybe . . ."

Laughton nodded as Kir reappeared, and Miss Enright visibly relaxed some. It made sense. Robot destroys Carl's arm and leg. Carl wants revenge on all of robot-kind, writes a killer program, and then someone killed him for it. But not to get rid of it, to use it? If they both wanted to use it, why kill him?

"He ever talk about his partner?" Laughton said.

"No."

"Did he ever say anything about having met someone that could help him, getting even with the robots?" Kir said.

She shook her head. "Just that the robots couldn't live without him. He took pleasure in that, how they needed his work. How pathetic he thought they were."

Just one of those hackers who saw the sims trade as another way to lord human superiority over the robots, that they needed something from him, that he could control them. Definitely would further suggest a tie between this case and Kir's; whoever wrote a deadly sim was probably a human supremacist.

Laughton waited a moment again to see if she would add anything. This all gave them a sense of who Smythe was, what kind of man, and it meshed with the picture he'd formed in his mind. But it wasn't giving him anything to go on. After it was clear she wouldn't talk, he held up his phone. "I want you to call us if you think of anything else."

Miss Enright stood up, and crossed to the counter to retrieve her phone. She held it out, and they tapped them together to exchange information. She got shy then, looking at the children, using them as an excuse not to meet his eye, or Kir's. "I'll show you out," she said after an awkward silence, and took a step forward. Laughton turned to let her pass him and she led the way down to the front door, less concerned about leaving the children alone than with Kir.

At the door, without meeting their eyes, she said, "Please don't talk to Bobby."

She was ashamed, not afraid of her husband's reaction. All of that trouble to get the subpoena, and he'd gotten nothing. "We'll try," Laughton said.

Her shoulders relaxed. "Thank you." She was truly grateful.

"I'm sorry for your loss," he said.

"Thanks," she said, but with little more feeling than if he had held a door open for her.

Outside, Laughton said, "Not much."

"The kids are nice," Kir said.

"Hmph," Laughton grunted, not amused. He pulled open the driver's-side door to his truck and stepped up inside.

Kir got in on the other side. "It was a mistake for me to come," the robot said. "I freaked her out."

Laughton tapped the screen of the GPS, turning it on, but his hand hovered there as he tried to decide where they should go next. "Nah, I should have thought of that. It's not going to be like it was. The people who moved here, they want to get away from you bastards."

"That's why I need you," he said.

"No kidding. That's why you always needed me. But I'm not moving to Washington, so don't even start that again."

The old argument filled the truck for a moment. Their ability to communicate with each other had been legendary—Laughton's skill at reading micro-expressions, and Kir's at reading Laughton, not just the basic hand signals they'd developed, but actually reading Laughton's face based on thousands of hours of footage, gave them an enormous edge. Working separately was almost like working with half a brain, but Laughton's days weren't supposed to be handling anything more complicated than drunken bravado, and Kir's weren't supposed to be filled with many humans.

"So you want to check out the husband?" Kir said.

"We probably should, just to cross it off," he said, opening the police database on the car's touch screen, "but the thing with cutting the arm and leg open doesn't scan. When I told her Smythe was a cyborg, she was shocked. I doubt her husband would have known." He tried Bobby Enright, then Robert Enright without luck. His phone buzzed, and he looked. It was from Kir. File photo of Robert Enright. He looked at his ex-partner. "Don't you see I'm doing it here?"

"I just got it first."

Laughton felt a surge of exasperation that he had to make a conscious effort to control. It sent a new wave of tingles across his left cheek. He put his fingertips to his temples. He opened the file Kir had forwarded. "I don't recognize the guy, and this doesn't have anything other than this address."

"Should we wait?"

"I'll put Dunrich on it." He tapped "Work" on the GPS, and the truck started backing out of the driveway. "Might as well go back to the station. See if anything's come in."

"Sounds like a plan," Kir said.

Didn't sound like much of anything.

Dunrich stood as Laughton and Kir entered the station. Laughton mentally rolled his eyes. Dunrich was fine on day-to-day things, but so far this case had revealed his limitations, and the chief didn't want to deal with more incompetence just then.

"Chief," the junior officer said, stepping around his desk, laptop computer in hand. "I found the hacker from TV."

Laughton stopped short and looked at his junior officer, incredulous. "How?"

Dunrich was at his side now, showing the chief a social media page for someone calling himself Crisper, no last name. Or maybe it was no first name. The profile picture showed a man from the neck down to his midbelly wearing a black T-shirt with white writing in an old command-prompt font that read "Alignment Lawful." All that could be gleaned from that was that the bit of skin visible at the neckline was white.

Dunrich kept stealing looks at Kir as the chief took in the page. "I called the station to see if Kara Letts would reveal her source," he explained.

"You got Kara Letts on the phone?" The chief was still shocked.

"I might have threatened to get a warrant," he said, glancing at Kir again, then down in embarrassment.

Laughton realized he should introduce them. "This is my old partner, Kir. Kir, Officer Dunrich."

"Hi," Dunrich said.

"Nice to meet you," Kir said.

Laughton steered them back to the case. "You threatened the warrant, and she told you . . ."

"No," Dunrich said, refocused, excited to show off. "She cited a whole bunch of court cases or something saying she didn't have to reveal her sources, but she slipped in the middle and said, 'I wouldn't tell you if I could,' so that made me think *she* didn't even know who her source was. So I thought, how could he have gotten in touch, and I started going back through Letts's social media accounts looking for someone contacting her with information, and this one jumped out. He made first contact this morning, the shirt's some old computer game reference, and he asked to be given rights to private message her."

Laughton raised his eyebrows. "That's amazing," he said, nodding.

Dunrich grinned, all his orbital muscles crinkling, looking almost like he wanted to laugh, he was so proud.

"See if you can get him to respond," Laughton said.

"I sent a message and a friend request," Dunrich said. "I said I was looking into the murder. I figure he was willing to talk to the press about it, he might just like the attention."

That's not how Laughton would have played it, but they'd have to wait and see now. "Good work."

"Right." Dunrich started for his desk, then turned back. "Oh, call came for you, Chief."

Laughton waited.

Dunrich went back to his desk, and checked the tablet there. "Uh, Cindy Smythe."

"Goddamn it!" Laughton said, his goodwill evaporating. "Why the hell didn't you call me?"

Dunrich blinked at him, unprepared for such a quick change of mood.

Laughton could feel his anger was out of proportion but, like with Erica, wasn't able to curb it. "Or forward me the message!"

Dunrich was still stunned to silence, confused how praise a moment before had shifted to yelling. He probably didn't even know why Laughton was so angry. And the thought made Laughton realize that he was angry at Dunrich, yes, but angry at himself too, because he'd forgotten about tracking Smythe's sister, and it was just another mistake piled on all the others he'd made in this investigation, and with help like Dunrich—one good thing out of how many dumb ones?—he couldn't afford to make mistakes. "Did you at least talk to her? Get a statement?"

"She wanted—"

"Forward me the fucking message," Laughton said. "Always forward me all my messages."

"But you've said to not forward anything that wasn't an emergency."

"And now I'm saying forward me everything." Laughton went into his office. There was too much blocking the door to slam it, so he left it opened. Kir leaned against the doorjamb. Laughton's phone buzzed, and Cindy Smythe's contact info popped up. He yelled from his desk, "Did she say anything about when it was a good time to call her?"

There was a delay, and Laughton was getting ready to get up and scream some more when Dunrich's answer came back, "No."

Kir said, "He did just do some real detective work."

"Kir, you don't know. You just don't."

Laughton looked at the time on the top of his phone screen: almost a quarter to four, or one on the West Coast. He tapped on the message, and then hit the icon for a video call. He hated doing interviews over the phone. It was so hard to read people, not being able to see their body language, and even in high definition, a face on a screen just wasn't the same as a face in person, especially since their eyes were always downturned, looking at the screen and not the camera. He saw himself doing that now, his own face filling the screen as the phone rang. He was looking to see if he looked as terrible as he felt, but only someone who knew him well would notice.

At last, a ring stopped midtrill, the sound of a mic going live came through as his face was relegated to a small box in the lower right-hand corner of the screen. After a delay, a young woman's face appeared. The little of her shoulders that were visible filled her shirt with the unnatural bulkiness of an exoskeleton. He could only imagine what her full body looked like. No wonder she chose to live off-preserve. Even on the phone, he could see that she'd been crying, the bags under her eyes puffy, her nose red. "Hello," she said as she registered the chief's face.

"Miss Smythe. My name is Jesse Laughton. I'm chief of police in Liberty on the SoCar Preserve."

"Hello," she said again.

"I'm calling about your brother."

She nodded.

corners of lips turned down, eyes narrowed to slits—anguish

She was going to cry again, Laughton thought, but she managed to hold off. "Can you talk now?" he said. "Do you think you can talk?"

She nodded, but didn't risk an attempt to actually speak.

"When was the last time you spoke to your brother?"

She closed her eyes, collecting herself, and when she opened them again, she looked tired instead of crushed. She took a deep breath before speaking. "Last Saturday, not this one just

four days ago, the one before that. I try to call Carl every weekend, but he doesn't always pick up and he never calls back."

"So, did you call this past weekend and he didn't pick up?"

"No, I was organizing a CBHC demonstration."

The Cyborg-Human Coalition was a fringe human rights
group that put an emphasis on equal cyborg rights within the
context of human rights. They had been one of the lobbying
organizations instrumental in the creation of the preserve system, but most members were dissatisfied with the inequality
they still saw on the preserves that were established. They tried
to ally themselves with the groups that represented peoples
of color, but those minorities were just as prejudiced against
cyborgs who they saw as voluntarily choosing to be part of
an outcast minority, as opposed to the challenge of being
born that way. They had little sympathy for people like Cindy
Smythe, for whom becoming a cyborg had not been a choice.
The most militant orgo groups, of course, would maintain that
she should have accepted being paralyzed. The CBHC's focus
had turned to the creation of a separate preserve on the West
Coast that they hoped would be more open-minded, given the
much larger cyborg population.

"Was your brother involved in the CBHC?" Laughton
asked.

Cindy Smythe shook her head. "Carl did everything he
could to hide the fact that he was a cyborg. He wanted nothing to do with the CBHC. He felt he could get back at society
other ways."

"Get back at society?" Laughton resisted the urge to look at
Kir. He didn't want to let Smythe know he wasn't alone. "What
did he mean?"

"You know we were hit by robots when we were younger?"

"We were told there was a car malfunction."

"No malfunction, and we weren't in a car. Some robots purposely ran us down when we were crossing the street. They'd taken the car off auto, and had been looking for humans to hit, because why not? It's not like they got in trouble for it or anything."

There was bitterness there, edged with anger. It seemed more directed at the fact that robots could do that kind of thing with impunity than over the result of the attack: the death of her mother, the loss of her ability to walk, and what Laughton was starting to really understand, the poisonous rage that consumed her brother. It seemed most likely it was the last that got him killed. His artificial arm and leg was the lesser of the two outcomes.

He adopted the use of Smythe's first name to keep it personal for her. "You said that Carl had ways other than joining protest groups to get back at robots?"

She tilted her head. "You know what he did, right?"

"Yes," Laughton said, but he wanted to hear her say it.

"He liked sims because it meant he was controlling them, you know, everything they were experiencing, how they were able to act. He was playing them like puppets, it was that power that he liked. And taking money off of them, not that he used it for anything. I was proud that he was working at least, when most humans just sit around letting the government take care of them. I guess that's taking their money too, you could say, but I think it's more like being kept as pets."

"Did he talk to you about sims, about people he worked with, names, places, anything?"

"I know Sam, of course"—she shook her head—"but otherwise, he never did more than allude to his work. Usually he sounded distant, and I knew he was just waiting until he could get off the phone."

"When you talked to him last, did he seem like he expected something coming up?"

"No. Like I said, I could barely get him to talk most of the time. I just liked to know he was still okay," she said, and her voice broke, her face flooded with the pain she'd been suppressing. "I'm all alone now," she said, her voice tight and high-pitched.

"I'm sorry to put you through this," he said. He knew that was trite, but it was what you said. He gave her a moment to come back to their conversation, but she was lost in a memory.

"Have you spoken to Sam?"

She shook her head, suppressing her tears, unable to speak. He wasn't going to get any more out of her. Living on the other side of the country, she didn't know anything anyway.

"If you think of anything else—"

"Had they really cut open his arm?" she said, almost a hiccough.

"Yes."

She closed her eyes and sighed. When she opened them again, she was more centered. "Carl would have hated that," she said. "He always thought he was weak for keeping it, that he should be true to his beliefs and live without an arm and leg, but"—and she smiled a knowing smile—"it's hard to live with a disadvantage. It's hard enough for us orgos as it is."

The self-pity made Laughton uncomfortable. "Thank you for calling, Miss Smythe."

"Find who did this. And I hope to god it was a robot. The last thing we need are orgos killing each other."

Laughton didn't want to get pulled into a political discussion. "Okay, then. I will. We'll keep you posted."

"Okay."

"Goodbye."

He hit the end button. The station phone was already ring-ing, but it cut off as Dunrich answered it out in the main room.

"Not much better than Enright," Kir said.

"It's like these guys were a pair of recluses," Laughton said. He heard the sound of the officer's chair sliding back, and then Dunrich looked in his office. "That was Marni, across the street at the Liberty Tavern. Caleb Mathieson got drunk and pulled a knife."

"Goddamn it. Was anyone hurt?"

"He wasn't even fighting with anyone. Just pulled the knife and waved it around. I'm going over to pick him up."

"Fine. Okay."

"Figured I'd just take him home."

"Works for me," Laughton said.

Dunrich nodded, then paused, seeming on the verge of say-ing something, but he didn't like something about the way the chief looked, and in the end backed out of the office in silence.

Feeling guilty, the chief called him back.

Dunrich looked in.

"Good work before," he said. "With the hacker. See if you can find Bobby Enright when you're done with Caleb."

Dunrich nodded, his features softening. He left without saying anything more.

Idiot Caleb Mathieson. Pulled shit like this at least once a week. Someday somebody's going to get hurt. If only Farrah would hold him in check, but she was drunk out of her mind half the time too. She just liked to do her drinking in private.

Despite his frustration with the Mathiesons, Laughton wished that he was the one going down to pick up Caleb, to go back to that being the biggest event of the day. He wished he could just turn over this homicide to someone else. He'd left Baltimore to get away from catching bodies.

Kir said, "What do you want to do now?"

"I want to get in bed," Laughton said.

Kir didn't respond.

"I should probably eat something," Laughton said.

The outer door banged open. "Chief!"

"I'm in here," Laughton called.

"Chief." Mathews appeared in the doorway. He pulled up when he saw Kir.

"Mathews, Kir; Kir, Mathews. He was my partner in Baltimore."

Mathews held out his hand. "Pleased to meet you," he said.

Kir shook. "Likewise."

Mathews said, "Those women you sent me to interview didn't know anything. They'd each met Smythe only once. One of them couldn't even really remember him at all. She kept saying, 'Are you sure? The guy that was killed? Are you sure?'"

No surprises there. Nobody knew these guys. "How'd the tech guys make out at the house?"

Mathews shook his head. "They said it could be days before they could find anything. They were actually pretty excited about it."

"And the robots?" Kir said. "The ones staking out the place?"

"They took off when the tech boys showed up."

"Did you get their plate?"

"Didn't match the model they were in."

"Of course not," Laughton said.

"What do you want me to do?" Mathews said. "Where's Dunrich?"

"Taking Caleb Mathieson home."

"I guess life goes on," Mathews said.

"That it does," Laughton said.

The outer door banged open again. "Chief!"

"Jesus, what is this?" Laughton said. "Yeah, I'm in here," he called.

Mathews had to squeeze farther into the room to allow Dunrich to come in. "He responded, Chief," Dunrich said.

Who? Laughton thought for a second, then said, "The hacker."

"Crisper," Dunrich said, waving his phone like he was holding the man right there.

Then a face peeked over Dunrich's shoulder. "Hiya, Jesse," the man said.

"Jesus, Dunrich, I thought you were taking Caleb home."

"But then this came in, and I thought . . ."

"Hey, are you a—" Caleb said to Kir, who answered, "Yes."

"You got a robot on the Preserve, Jesse?" Caleb said.

"Get him out of here, Dunrich."

"But Crisper. Willing to meet in person in Beaufort in an hour. I thought I could go."

"No, you're not going to go. You're going to take Caleb home. Like you were supposed to. Mathews, go with him." *Let Dunrich be Mathews's problem for a little while,* Laughton thought. "See if you can find Bobby Enright. Robert. His wife was having a relationship with Smythe. But he supposedly didn't know about it, so if you can sound him out without telling him . . ."

"Right," Mathews said.

"You." Laughton pointed at Dunrich. "Text me the details. I'm going to see the hacker."

"You all know there's a robot right here," Caleb Mathieson said. "There's a robot on the fucking Preserve."

"Get him out of here," Laughton said.

Mathews started walking toward the door, forcing Dunrich and Mathieson back. "Come on. Come on."

Dunrich looked like he was almost going to cry as he was

shuffled out of the office. "This was my lead, Chief. You should let me come."

"He's got a fucking robot in there," Caleb Mathieson was saying from out in the squad room.

Kir said, "We could let him come."

"No," Laughton snapped. He stood up, and went to the door. The three men were heading out the front.

The text came through a second later. The meeting was at the national cemetery in Beaufort. "We're on our way to Beaufort," he said to Kir, opening the contact list on his phone. "I better check in with Tommy Tantino first. He's chief of police down there."

"All right."

Tantino picked up himself. "Police?"

"They have you answering phones out there now?" Laughton said.

"Jesse. Jesus. You sure hit the jackpot. What's happening?"

It was real concern in Tantino's voice. They'd spoken over the phone a few times in the last nine months and met in person twice, and Jesse really liked him. Former New York City police, a good guy. "I'm on my way onto your turf. Meeting an informant. Hacker. Based out your way."

"Name?" Tantino said.

"Just an online handle: Crisper. I was hoping you could tell me more."

"Means nothing to me. Can't think who that would be."

"You got names for any of your hackers?" Laughton said.

"I treat that as 'don't ask, don't tell,'" Tantino said. "I know there's some sims business, but I'm busy enough worrying about local crime to worry about that. We've got a couple of groups that like to fight when they're drunk, which is always. I think it's just entertainment for them."

That sounded about right, Laughton thought.

"You want some backup while you're here?" Tantino said.

"I don't want to scare the guy off," Laughton said. "It's got to be me."

"I hear you," Tantino said. "This murder sucks. Puts everyone on edge."

"Tell me about it."

"Place was a beautiful dream, wasn't it? Guess we should have expected a wake-up call."

"Drinking and fighting's not much of a dream."

"Small price for kids playing with other kids."

Laughton tried to measure the two against each other. He wasn't sure the math worked out. "I guess we can only hope they'll learn a different way," he said, thinking about Betty and her school.

"All we've got is the future," Tantino said.

"Plenty of ways to muck it up today."

There was a pause as both men thought about that. Jesse wondered when he had gotten so cynical. One of his main gripes with his father was the way he disparaged Jesse's optimism. But in this case, maybe it was evidence that the preserve *had* been a dream, and that robots were not humanity's problem. It was each other.

"We just do our best," Tantino said.

"What else you going to do?" Laughton said.

"Well, Jesse," Tantino said, "you let me know if you need any help."

"Will do."

"Call anytime."

"Thanks, Tommy." Laughton broke the call. To Kir, he said, "He's got our back if we need him."

"We're going to be late for Erica," Kir said.

"Half hour there, half hour back, maybe an hour with the informant: should be plenty of time before picking up Erica."

"Just as long as you tell Betty I tried to tell you."

"I'm ignoring you," Laughton said, heading out the door.

"I'm not the one you have to worry about," Kir said.

"Are you kidding?" Laughton said. "I'm worried about everybody."

Beaufort had remained the picture of a southern town from several hundred years ago, the robots having turned it into a tourist destination, cultivating an image as Charleston's little brother. Large houses with screened-in porches fronted marshland. A historically preserved, brick downtown, built long ago around what was once an important harbor, had persisted, right up to the opening of the preserve, as a vibrant commercial center. Old robots, as they found themselves phased out, had congregated there, creating a quaint community that had added to the town's charm. The town had also been home to one of the larger human populations on the East Coast, a result of the military's former presence, a training camp and air base nearby. Unsurprisingly, the elderly robots were the ones who had been most resistant to relocation for the creation of the preserve, and their human neighbors had even argued for a dispensation, or more radically, to have the preserve's borderline drawn around the town. But it had proven too good an opportunity for the government to squeeze the elderly, seen as pathetic sponges by most of society, and many of the aged robots had chosen deactivation over relocation.

The cemetery was on Boundary Street, which must at one time in the distant past have been the northernmost road in town. Now if it served as a boundary at all, it was only between the northern and southern parts of town. A long, low brick wall ran along the street, protecting the dead from wayward visitors, or perhaps protecting any children walking by from imagined terrors. It was a national military cemetery, stark and imposing. The uniform white pillars that marked the graves were laid out in orderly rows, which played optical illusions as the truck drove by, almost like a Hoberman sphere, seeming to come together, expand outward, and come together again as the pillars lined up at different angles. The main entrance was flanked by two stone reliefs of the Seal of the United States, the self-divided bald eagle perpetually caught between war and peace. In the center of the road, a flagpole flew a worn, sun-bleached US flag at the customary half-mast.

Laughton took manual control of the truck, guiding it at a crawl up and down the roads that cut through the burial ground. He had never been in a cemetery before. Ever since the first plague, all humans were cremated. Looking at the vast number of monuments spread out around him now, it was hard to associate them with actual people. It was like an anti-septic garden filled with indifferent flora, pretty, but not particularly interesting to him. The noise of at least two lawn mowers driving themselves invisibly among the graves challenged the cemetery's silent gravity. He tried to make out his quarry, but nobody was visible anywhere.

"Getting anything?" Laughton asked Kir. The robot's thermal vision would see the hacker, even if he was hiding behind one of the many trees interspersed with the graves. Robots ran hot only in the head or the torso, but humans ran hot all over.

"No," the robot said.

Laughton checked the forwarded text from Crisper again. "He said the cemetery. And we're on time. Should I text him?"

"Give him time," Kir said.

The truck came to a sudden stop as what Laughton first took to be a bird almost hit the windshield. As it flitted around to the driver's-side window, Laughton saw that it was a quadcopter the size of a sparrow. "Goddamn it," Laughton said, mostly at the shock of having the truck's auto-safety measures wrest control of the truck from him. "Fucking idiot."

The drone hovered outside his window, a quarter-inch, spherical camera mounted to the top of the copter taking his measure before flying around to take a look at Kir.

"Flying robots are illegal here," Laughton said.

"All robots are illegal here," a voice said from some hidden speaker.

Kir put down his window and reached for the copter, but it flew out of his reach. "It's not a robot," he said.

"But you are," the voice from the drone said.

"Crisper?" Laughton called, leaning over Kir.

"What's with the metal?" the voice said. "Talk fast."

"He's assisting me in the murder investigation," Laughton said. "We were partners in Baltimore."

There was a pause. It could have been simply that Crisper was thinking, but it was more likely he was running them through facial recognition software. "Metal gets out here," he said at last.

Kir pushed the button to release the door, but Laughton put his hand on the robot's shoulder, stopping him from getting out. He called across his partner, "You said on the television you weren't afraid, and I thought, there's a reasonable man."

There was a pause. The whir of the quadcopter's rotors evoked the summer sound of a flitting bee.

"Or we could just have the conversation like this," Laughton said.

"Okay," the voice said. "Follow."

Kir pulled his door shut as Laughton resumed manual controls, crawling along behind the hovering vehicle.

"Smart," Kir said.

"Something," Laughton answered.

The drone led them back to the cemetery's main entrance. Across the street, there was another small plot with much older gravestones of various shapes and sizes. Standing in the shadow of a tree in the midst of the graves was a white-haired woman, bone thin, collarbone showing over her argyle-patterned strapless sundress. She wore lightweight virtual reality goggles, and held a phone in one hand out in front of her, no doubt using it as a remote control for the drone. As it reached her, she took off the goggles, and plucked the copter from the air.

Laughton pulled the truck to the curb, and the partners got out.

"Excellent voice modulator," Kir said as they approached the woman.

"Thank you," she said. Her real voice was light and warm, suffused with amusement that showed at the corners of her eyes. She turned her attention to the chief. "Jesse Laughton," she said, as though taking stock of him. It made Laughton long for his mother, which was not the best place from which to start an interview. He wondered why he hadn't heard from Betty about her mother.

Crisper looked back at Kir, her eyebrows lower, her jaw set forward. "I don't like having this one here."

"You don't mind," Kir said.

"Don't presume to tell me my own mind, robot." She was stern, but the light in her eyes belied any real anger. Still, Laughton was worried she might take off without stating her business.

"He's only here to assist," Laughton said. "He wants the same thing we do, to catch a murderer and get the robots off the preserve."

Crisper glared at Kir another moment, and then her features softened again as she turned back to Laughton, a hint of her initial amusement settling in. "Okay, you share first," she said.

"I'm sorry?" Laughton said, taken aback.

"You first," Crisper said. "Then we'll see."

"We can't discuss an ongoing investigation," Laughton said, at the same time Kir said, "What do you want to know?" Laughton bristled at being undermined, but swallowed his annoyance.

"Everything. Suspects. Motives. Whatever you've got."

"I'm sorry, Miss . . . ," Laughton said.

"Crisper will do."

"Miss Crisper, we're here because you said you had information for us."

"Patience," she said, which left Laughton anything but.

Kir took over again. He had further to go to earn her trust. "Carl Smythe was a sims hacker. Death by Taser. Cybernetic arm and leg cut open. No suspects, no witnesses. Partner Sam McCardy missing. Distributor Carter Jones missing."

"You know nothing," Crisper said.

"We know very little," Laughton said.

"So not only was the press conference a show, but it was a blind."

"We had nothing to do with that."

"That's clear," she said. "Even if your record didn't speak for itself, you show sense." She thought for a moment. "Carter's my distributor too. I'm sure he's not far. He lacks the courage to leave the preserve."

"So you write sims?" Laughton said, confirming it.

"I assume that's of no concern here," she said.

"Of course," Kir said.

"You don't have any say here," Crisper said to the robot.

"You said on the television," Laughton said, "you weren't worried for your own safety. Why?"

"Because it was the least I could do to reduce people's panic. You people weren't doing that."

"So you do fear for your safety?" Laughton said.

"I'll say I'm concerned by the whole thing."

"Well, if you're looking for reassurance here—"

She shook her head and clicked her tongue to stop him.

Laughton waited. Kir was silent.

"I never met Smythe. Did I say that already? But I know his work. You think Killer App is his," she said.

"That's the theory," Kir said. Somehow, despite the initial combativeness, the robot and the hacker had found an easier rapport than Laughton had managed.

"Mine too," Crisper said.

"The rest of the theory," Kir said, "is that that's what got him killed."

"It might seem like the only apparent motive."

"That or the cyborg angle," Laughton said.

She tutted again, chastising Laughton. "It's good I went against my better judgment here," she said.

Laughton, smarting at being swatted like a boy reaching for a fresh cookie from a still-hot baking sheet, said, "Titanium."

"Okay, big man," Crisper said. "Okay." She looked at her phone and held the drone open on her palm. Selecting something on the phone, the drone took off. Laughton and Kir both followed its path with their eyes as it disappeared between two trees. "Auto," Crisper said by way of explanation.

The police turned their attention back to her.

"I notice a few weeks ago that my sims were leaving the preserve in a new pattern."

"How," Laughton said.

"Tracker," Kir said.

"Ding, ding, ding. I put a tracker in anything I ever write. Lets me know exactly the impact I'm having."

"Don't the end-user robots see them?"

"Why should they care?" Crisper said. Then with a sly smile, "They don't find them anyway. They're not looking, and they'd be hard pressed to find them if they were." She paused to allow them to admire her skill, then continued, "Carter works for the Sisters. Did before the preserve—we all know each other going back—"

How far back, Laughton wondered. She was at least twice Carter's age, and he still didn't know who the Sisters were.

"My sims go from Carter to the Sisters, and then out by truck north and south." The drone returned then. Crisper took it, and removed a memory stick from a clip at the bottom. She handed it to Chief Laughton.

"This is . . . ?" he said, holding it up.

"Distribution map. You'll see what I'm talking about, and be able to follow to the source."

Laughton nodded, and pocketed it.

"So north and south," Kir said.

"Until a few weeks ago," Crisper said. "Then about half went that way, and half started leaving by boat through the harbor, and from a point out on the western edge of the preserve."

Jesse studied her face as she spoke, but there were none of the micro-expressions that gave away a lie through a flash of real emotion before the deliberate mask of a false one could be assumed. She was telling the truth.

"Titanium," Kir said.

She nodded once without saying anything.

"Why couldn't it be the Sisters changing it up?" Laughton said.

"Because she sees where it goes after it leaves the preserve too," Kir said.

"Carter's an idiot," Crisper said. "The Sisters didn't get where they are by being pretty. They got there by following in their father's footsteps, over bodies."

Was it that simple? Laughton thought. Just drug turf? Kir's case was unrelated? Laughton didn't think so.

"So Smythe was a message?" Laughton said.

"All I'm saying," Crisper said, "is that you might want to take a look at that map."

Laughton tried to figure out what was in it for this woman, why she was handing them the evidence that could take the whole operation down, kill sims entirely, for a little while, at least.

As though reading his mind, Crisper said, "Map's just like a sim. Plug and play, onetime use. You have about two minutes to view, and you won't have any luck with screenshots or photos."

"That good, huh?" Kir said.

"Smythe dead and Sam missing? The best," she said without an ounce of bragging in it.

"Thank you," Laughton said.

"You said it yourself, Jesse Laughton. We all want the same thing: catch a killer, eject some metals. Sims is sims." She addressed Kir, "Get the hell off our land, robot." With that, she turned and walked away.

"She likes you," Laughton said to Kir.

"What can I say? I have that effect on women."

Laughton snorted. "Metal bastard." They went back to the truck and got in. It was almost time to get Erica. He dug the memory stick that Crisper had given him out of his pocket and handed it to Kir. "You want to read this?"

"Are you crazy? Memory sticks are burning robots up. We'll wait until we can use a computer."

"Right," Laughton said, nodding. He rubbed his hands on his face. "My mind is fried."

"Seriously?" Kir said.

Jesse realized what he'd said. "Poor choice of words."

Kir said nothing. After a few seconds, he smiled and said, "Let's go get my niece."

"We're going to be late."

Jesse's phone buzzed. He looked at it. It was a text from Kir: "I told you so."

"You really just texted me?" he said to his partner.

Kir held his hands up innocently.

Laughton shook his head, and started the car.

The Liberty Primary and Secondary School was housed in a former strip mall on the highway out of town. Doors had been cut between each of the storefronts allowing for four sections, each containing a class spanning three ages. Erica was in the 7-8-9s, a class of sixteen students. Most of the children had never been in school before, human schools outside of the major cities nonexistent, and robot schools unnecessary when knowledge could be uploaded en masse.

Erica's classroom had been a clothing store at some time, and the walls were still covered in long horizontal slats from which hooks could be hung in endless configurations. A SMART Board hung on a side wall, and maps and wildlife photographs and children's art did its best to make the space feel like a proper classroom and not a failed business.

"I'm so sorry," Laughton said to Miss Holly as he and Kir came in the door, the young teacher already putting her bag over her shoulder, ready to go home.

"It's fine," Miss Holly said, but her tone made it clear she was annoyed.

Erica sat on the floor, engrossed in some kind of game on her tablet.

"Hey there, little one," Kir said.

At the sound of his voice, Erica looked up. Her face opened wide. "Kir!" She jumped up, ran to him, and threw her arms around the robot. "Kir, Kir, Kir." She released Kir's waist and grabbed his hand, and jumped up and down, up and down, jerking his arm.

Laughton could tell his old partner was pleased simply because he said nothing, allowing Erica to do her celebratory dance without comment. Laughton was happy too, happy and proud that his daughter had that kind of bond with a robot. Despite everything that was said around her, sometimes by her parents even, she was untroubled with prejudice, something too few people were, and the very reason the preserve existed. "Okay, Erica," Laughton said. "That's enough." She kept jumping and squealing. "Enough, Erica." He put his hand on her head and she stopped. She didn't let go of Kir's hand. Instead, she started to drag him into the classroom.

"I want to show you my nature project," she said, and took him over to a small table that was covered with shoebox dioramas.

Miss Holly came over, and said, "Is this your uncle?" to Erica. Getting a better look at Kir, her smile wavered, but she did what she could to hide it. Only Laughton would probably have noticed. It was amazing: when they lived among them, it could be a real challenge to tell the robots from the humans. Laughton guessed that months without seeing any robots made their appearance as "other" more apparent.

"An old friend," Kir said.

"Right," Miss Holly said, and whatever more she had planned to say, she kept to herself. "See you tomorrow, Erica."

"Can I just show him—"

"No," Laughton said.

Erica flashed an exaggerated grimace, and then started dragging Kir toward the front door.

"Say goodbye, Erica," Laughton called after her, but she didn't even look back. Laughton rolled his eyes at Miss Holly, and said, "Goodbye."

Miss Holly, restrained, said, "Have a good night."

———

At home, Erica gave Kir a tour of the house while Laughton took some Tylenol and ibuprofen. When they joined him in the kitchen, Kir said, "You should go to bed."

"No," Laughton said, "I'm not going to leave you."

"You look terrible," Kir said. "You'll be a greater help to me rested."

"You sure?" Laughton said. The idea of bed seemed so wonderful. It wasn't even beginning to get dark yet, but his head weighed a hundred pounds.

"Go."

"Kir will watch me," Erica said.

Laughton stood, but hesitated another moment. "I feel bad. You sure?"

"Go."

Laughton was grateful for his old partner. He put his hand on Kir's shoulder on the way out of the kitchen. "Be good for Uncle Kir," Laughton said to Erica. "Just make sure she eats," he said.

"I was going to plug her in," Kir said with a grin.

Upstairs in the darkened room, Laughton took his phone out of his pocket before taking off his pants. He climbed into bed, the pain in his head spinning around to his face as he lay, his head back, like a bubble in a bottle of water. The overhead fan was pleasantly chilling.

He felt guilty for leaving Erica. Betty would not approve. He reached over for his phone. Still no text from her. He texted, "ETA?"

This time, the phone indicated that she was typing back. Eventually the words popped up: "Soon. Everything's fine. Tell you about it when I get home."

He dropped the phone down on his nightstand, rubbed his face with both hands, and let out a long breath.

———

It was dark in the room when Laughton jolted awake. The phone on his nightstand was buzzing, Commissioner Ontero's name showing on the screen. Laughton closed his eyes, not wanting to pick up, but that only made him feel guilty. He turned, propped himself on one elbow on the bed, and picked up the phone. "Laughton," he said.

"Your boys' house just burnt down."

"What?" Jesse swung his feet around so he was sitting up. "Whose house?"

"Your dead hacker. Or it's still burning. I don't know."

"What are you talking about?"

"My computer boys were staying out there as their decryption programs ran. Thank god they were staying on the first floor."

Jesse's thoughts went to the robots who had been staking out the place earlier in the day. "What happened? Who started it?"

"You want to get out there. It's still going. They just called."

"Shit. Did they get anything out?"

"Jesse, are you hearing these boys could have been burnt up? What the fuck is going on?"

"I don't know."

"Well, find out. You and your partner need to come down here for a meeting tomorrow with all of the top brass."

"Waste of time," Laughton mumbled.

"Be there." And Ontero hung up.

Laughton stood up. His head felt heavy, but the discomfort in his face had faded to a small, nagging spot just below his left eye, manageable. He pulled his pants back on, almost tripping. Erica's door was slightly ajar. He shone his phone in the gap and saw her calm form sprawled out on her back in bed, one arm draped across her forehead. He started down the stairs, hearing voices. When he came into the dining room, he found Betty and Kir sitting across from one another at the dining room table. Betty looked disheveled and exhausted.

"I'm so glad we don't live in Charleston," she said when she saw him.

"Sam and Smythe's house is on fire," he said to Kir.

"What!"

"Ontero wouldn't give details, but I'm guessing the anti-hacking program wasn't bullshit. We should go."

"Now?" Betty said.

Laughton came up behind her, bent to wrap an arm around her, and kissed the top of her head. "How's your mom?"

"She's fine. I set her up in the guest room. It took forever in the emergency room, and then they wanted us to see a dentist about the broken teeth, but he said that he wanted the swelling to go down before he assessed what needed to be done. We can talk later if you need to go."

Kir stood up, and Betty did as well.

"Okay," she said. She stretched. "I've got to deal with a roomful of terrors in the morning. Time to go to bed."

"Good night," Kir said.

"Good night, hon," Laughton said.

She kissed him on the cheek as she walked out, and the former partners were left in the dining room in the small area lit by the overhead light. It was a bit like being in an interrogation room.

"We better go," Kir said.

"Commissioner demands our presence in a roomful of our

own terrors in the morning, some bigwig metals conference."

"Got it from Pattermann," Kir said.

"All right." Laughton thought about those robots hanging around the hackers' house. The fire might have been caused by Smythe's security, or it might have been something else. "One minute," he said, and headed into the kitchen. He pulled open the basement door beside the refrigerator. Brooms and mops and brushes clattered on their hooks on the back of the door as he went downstairs. The basement was split in half, the front finished with wall-to-wall carpeting and a drywall ceiling with high-hat lights. They had set it up as a den with the same furniture and television that had graced their apartment in Baltimore—no looting the preserve for the chief of police's family. Laughton went through the hollow-core door into the back half of the basement, which was unfinished, a storage area and workbench lit by bare lightbulbs, the sockets screwed into the joists below the exposed underfloor. There was a safe under the workbench, a green, two-foot cube, with both a keypad and a manual dial. His mind blanked on the combination for a moment, his eyes going up and to the right as he tried to remember.

The combo clicked in his mind, and he spun the dial, right, left, right, and a red LED light began to blink next to the keypad. He punched in the code, and the light turned green, the sound of the lock disengaging, a dull thunk. He pulled the safe open and took out two electromagnetic dampers, black disks maybe two and a half inches across and half an inch thick with a recessed button on the top to arm them. The damper would attach itself to a robot, and override its system, effectively shutting him down for as long as ten minutes with no lasting effect. He pocketed those. Then he pulled out a shoulder holster that contained a Taser on the left and a yellow, fingerprint-locked service revolver, his spare, the other one still in the drawer at the station. He slung his arms through the straps, adjusting the holster so it fit comfortably. He hadn't needed to carry any weapons in the past nine months, but he had still kept them in working order, cleaning and checking them once a month. He considered the magazines of electric-tipped bullets at the bottom of the safe, but he decided the dampers were enough if they ran into any robots. He closed the safe, and it locked itself.

Upstairs, Laughton saw Kir see the weapons, but his partner didn't comment. He just followed Laughton to the front door.

The fire had run its course by the time Chief Laughton's truck pulled up to the house. The smoky, acrid smell made Jesse cough as he got out of the truck.

A tall man with hair past his shoulders and a beard that ran halfway down his chest was leaning against a sedan on the other side of the street. He had presumably been watching the fire. "You missed the fun," he called over to them.

Jesse crossed the street. "You the tech guy?"

"One of them," the man said. He jerked a thumb toward the car he was leaning against. "Zach is in the car. He's panicked that breathing in any of the shit from the fire's going to kill him."

"It might," Kir said.

The man shrugged. "I'm not worried about it. I hate to be a stickler, but you've got some ID?"

Jesse and Kir each flashed their badges. "Jesse Laughton, chief of police in Liberty. This is Detective Kir from Health and Human Services."

"Hence the public health warning," the man said.

Kir nodded, noncommittal.

"I'm Jeremy." He turned and opened the door. "Hey, Zach, get out here."

The driver's-side door opened, and a small man with tight curly hair cut close to his head appeared. "Hi," he said.

"What happened in there?" Laughton said.

"First off, there are like eight hundred computers in there," Jeremy said.

"Maybe fifty," Zach said from his place on the other side of the car.

"I was in there earlier," Laughton said. "I saw."

"Well, they're all password protected, so we started running password breakers on them."

"On all of them?"

"Eventually," Jeremy said. "Took most of the day."

"Whatever encryption they're using is sick," Zach said, and the glow of admiration in his voice was obvious. "Normal people, it takes maybe five, ten minutes for the programs to break in. These have been running for hours."

"Could running all of those programs have caused the fire?" Laughton said. "Overheating?"

Jeremy shrugged. "Well, it *could* have."

"But not likely," Kir said.

Laughton looked across at the house he had been in less than twenty-four hours earlier. The structure was more or less intact. The windows had blown out and part of the roof had collapsed, a jagged mess of solar panels jutting out of the top of the house.

"So what happened?" Jesse said.

Jeremy said, "We'd crashed out on the floor in the living room. There was nothing we could do while the programs ran."

"Something woke me," Zach said, finally having come around the car to join them. "I don't know what. A noise."

"That server room up front was glowing, like orange light. We were like, shit, and got the hell out of there."

"This sound," Laughton said, "could it have been someone starting the fire? Maybe throwing something in from outside?"

Zach shook his head. "I don't even know if it was a sound."

"I didn't hear anything," Jeremy said. "Not that that means anything. You think someone torched the place?"

"My officer Mathews saw some robots hanging around out front this morning."

"Yeah, he mentioned that," Zach said.

"We haven't seen anyone, but we've mostly been inside," Jeremy said.

"Did you find anything before the fire?" Kir said.

Zach shook his head. "We couldn't get at anything."

Jeremy said, "I think our program cracked in, and that some booby trap started the fire."

Laughton looked at Kir, but his partner was focused on the two tech specialists.

"You get your stuff out?" Kir said.

"It's all in the car. Just a couple of laptops."

Kir reached into his pocket, and held something out to them. "Can you help us with this?" he said. "It's plug and play, auto-execute. Supposed to auto-delete after a few minutes."

"Sim?" Jeremy said, taking it. Zach opened the rear door of the car, retrieving a computer.

"No," Kir said. "Data. We don't know what. But we don't want to risk anything."

Jeremy handed it over to Zach, who had the computer balanced on the trunk of the car. He was typing away. "Give me a minute to set up some protections."

"Let's go look in the house," Laughton said.

"Don't open it without us," Kir said to the tech boys. Jeremy had joined his partner at the computer screen. They were already caught up in their new challenge.

Laughton and Kir crossed the street. "It's not safe to go in there," Kir said.

"We're not going to do a full search or anything. I want to see if there's an obvious cause to the fire."

The banks of solar panels closest to the house were black-

ened, and burnt with solidified drips of plastic running off
their edges. Heat was still radiating off of the house. The tech
team had left the front door open when they had retreated.
Lawton pulled out his phone and kicked on the flashlight.

Kir stepped in first, and Laughton followed right behind
him. He coughed as the soot and smoke stung his eyes and the
back of his throat. Kir turned to him. "You okay?"

Laughton was still coughing, but he managed to squeeze
out an "I'm fine." He stepped past his partner into the server
room, scanning the floor back and forth with his flashlight,
looking for the broken glass of a homemade firebomb or a
brick or rock used to break a window, but there was nothing.
The shelves that the servers had been housed on had burned,
causing them to all fall into the bottom of the shelving's metal
frames, a melted mass of blackened plastic.

Kir went over to the shelves, squatting so he could look at
the destroyed computers.

"See something?" Laughton said.

"No," Kir said, standing. "But the degree to which these
melted, I bet it was one of these that started it."

"Wouldn't you have to make hardware alterations to cause
it to burn?"

"First," Kir said, "they might have. But if you're as brilliant
as this guy's supposed to have been, you shut down the fans,
overpower the system, causing enough heat, you can definitely
fry the machine, maybe catch it on fire."

"Let's look around more," Laughton said, starting out of
the room.

"Not you," Kir said, and Laughton turned back to look at
him.

"What do you mean, not me?"

"There's nothing to see here, and you know it. No reason to

risk anything. Check on how they're doing with that memory stick."

"Like you can't be hurt either?"

"I'm easier to fix."

Laughton shook his head. "No," he said, and headed back toward the living room. The paint on the walls had blistered, and chipped. The floors were covered in soot and ash. The cabinets in the kitchen had started to fall off the wall, lurching at a disconcerting angle. The living room was a mass of black. All of the computers had burned here too. Seeing the melted gaming consoles was painful. Most of the books seemed intact, but when Laughton picked one up, it fell apart in his hands. "So much for getting anything from here."

"You want to go upstairs too?" Kir said. "Feel like falling through a floor?"

"Okay," Laughton said. "Jesus."

Laughton didn't realize how hot it had been in there until he stepped back out into the cool night air. He felt a layer of sweat drying on his forehead. It was a relief.

They joined the two hackers at their car. "We've set up a firewall that will prevent the program from auto-executing and give us a chance to scan it for malware or maybe get some idea of what it is before we open it."

"Ready?" Zach said over his shoulder to Laughton and Kir.

"Yes," Kir answered.

Zach plugged the memory stick into the side of his computer. A file name appeared on the screen, but nothing else happened. Then a bar appeared that began to fill in, in green.

"Is that something?"

"Virus scan," Jeremy said.

The bar finished filling. "That was fast."

"Must be a small file," Jeremy said.

"Should we run it?" Zach said.

"Do it."

The cursor on the screen moved over to the file name, and clicked.

Instantly, a satellite map of the preserve appeared on-screen. Then an overlay of lines traced out roads. The camera followed one of those roads out to the western edge of the reservation. The camera then panned back east until it had reached Charleston and the harbor. The line continued over the water. Then the screen went black.

Zach started typing, but the screen remained blank. "What the hell," he said.

"You get that?" Laughton said to Kir.

"I've got it," Kir said.

"What the goddamn hell," Zach said.

"It fry your computer?" Laughton said.

The screen flickered back to life. "No," Zach said, the relief audible as he exhaled.

"You waiting out here?" Laughton said.

"Commissioner said to wait for you, then whatever you want."

"Go home," Laughton said. "There's nothing more out here. Thanks for your work."

"You need anything else?" Zach said. "Like this." He handed the memory stick back to Kir.

"I think we're all right," Kir said. Laughton wasn't sure if they had tumbled to the fact that Kir was a robot.

"All right," he said, opening the passenger-side door to the car.

Laughton and Kir stepped back. As the car pulled away, Laughton said, "I saw one of those routes went out west, past here."

"Santee."

"Santee? Where the fuck is Santee?"

"Resort town off of Lake Marion."

"I don't know what the hell you're talking about," Laughton said. "Is that even on the preserve?"

"Right on the western border."

"There's no one out there. Liberty's as west as you get."

"If there's no one out there, that seems like a good place to be smuggling sims."

"Shit," Laughton said. It felt like the net was widening instead of tightening. At this stage in an investigation, even if he had no idea about what happened, he had usually identified who was involved, but with this, it seemed to just be going farther and farther afield.

"You can sleep on the way there," Kir said, assuming that was Laughton's hesitation.

"Who needs sleep?" Laughton said.

"I certainly don't, meatbag," Kir said.

"Just wait. I'll put you to sleep," Laughton said. Sleep would be nice, but it was the least of his concerns at that moment.

"We'll see who's asleep when we get there."

"I guess we will," Laughton said.

Darkness coated them. They were out on one of the old county highways. Kir had entered the destination based on what he'd seen on Crisper's map, and the truck was driving.

"You know where we're going?" Laughton said.

"Checked it on satellite."

"And?"

"Someone's out there."

"Great," Laughton said.

The undercarriage lights that lit the guidelines on the road so the truck could stay on track cast an aura of light on which they floated. Everything beyond that thin halo of blurred pavement was shades of black. It was oppressive, like being caught in an out-of-service elevator. What Laughton knew must be beautiful South Carolina fields was a great unknown. Back in the day, there must have been some electric lights visible, streetlights or isolated farmhouses, barns, but now it was just void. No wonder the robots had turned this land over to the humans. It was of no value to them. Robots were hardly a rural race.

As though reading his thoughts, Kir said, "So how's this great preserve experience really going? As a human, living on the inside."

"Dull." Laughton thought more on it. "Depressing. Everyone here's just waiting to die, drinking their way through. Only crime I have to deal with are drunks, and that's all day every day. It's like I'm a principal in some giant outdoors high school."

"If you're the principal, then I'm the superintendent."

"Fighting for us lowly humans so we can drink ourselves to extinction on our own land."

"Something like that," Kir said.

"Betty's doing the real important work here," Laughton said. "If you think perpetuating the human race is important. I don't know."

"Yeah."

"Evolution's supposed to be survival of the fittest. We're no longer the fittest."

"No other species built their replacement."

Laughton gave up trying to see outside. He closed his eyes, and the faint hiss of the tires on the pavement was the only thing that let him know they were still moving.

"Head?" Kir said.

"Just tired," the chief said without opening his eyes. Kir remained silent, and Laughton tried to empty his mind. Instead of feeling anxious about not knowing where he was or being able to see, he tried to focus on his breathing, something Betty had tried to teach him years ago that he continued to attempt but never found to work. Instead, feeling the presence of his partner, he said, "I'm not asleep."

"I know."

"You better not be reading my heartbeat."

"How long have I known you? I know not to read your vitals. I was just giving you a chance to rest before we go do this thing."

The interchange was so familiar, it comforted Laughton in a way he didn't know he needed to be comforted. Maybe he'd made a mistake when he decided to move to the preserve instead of the Department of Health and Human Services. Maybe this wasn't the best way to serve and protect. But his mind always came around to Betty's work, and Erica's well-being, and he figured he could make do with drunks for them.

Laughton opened his eyes, and rubbed his face with both hands. He sat up. Still an envelope of shadow around them, although there was a scattering of stars visible now. The sight of them caused a small leap in his chest. He'd never seen stars before the preserve, and they still got to him with a little boy's excitement. Erica would have that. Erica *did* have that.

"There," Kir said.

Laughton looked off to the right and saw the eerie glow of electric lights in the distance. "What's that?"

"I don't know."

The truck turned off on a narrow, two-lane road, its pavement a network of cracks and fault lines, the asphalt a loose puzzle that made a street. A sign read "Lake Marion Country Club."

"Someone's out here, and they're not making an effort to hide it."

As they got closer, the lights differentiated into a handful of buildings. The largest was an oversize rendition of a traditional southern plantation house with white columns, and a front porch that stretched across both wings. Most likely built in the twentieth century, its other anachronism, besides its enormous footprint, was plate glass windows between the columns, which afforded a view straight through the opulent lobby and its crystal chandelier to another set of floor-to-ceiling plate glass windows that must have looked out on the enormous lake behind the clubhouse. The smaller buildings looked as though they had served as storage sheds, garages, and powerhouses in the distant past.

The GPS announced, "You have arrived," and Laughton took manual control to guide it into a parking space across from the main entrance. The lot was full of a wide variety of cars. Clunkers with rusty gashes and missing hubcaps were parked next to squat, angular sports cars worth more than Laughton made in a year.

No one was out front, nor could anyone be seen in the part of the lobby that was visible. "Seems awfully quiet for so many lights," Laughton said.

"There are humans here," Kir said, using his thermal vision.

"Freaky metal bastard," Laughton said.

"Flesh face," Kir shot back.

" 'Flesh face'? Really?"

Kir shrugged. "You turned it personal."

"But 'flesh face'?"

They headed for the front entrance. If anyone here was worried about security, their truck had no doubt been spotted the second they turned into the drive. There was no reason to sneak in. As they started up the few stairs to the porch, a figure walked into the lobby from the left. The bend of his shoulders made him human. He must have caught some movement out of the corner of his eye, because he looked their way, and Laughton, stunned, recognized Jones, the missing sims runner. Jones made him at the same time, his eyes going wide. He began to run.

Laughton jumped up the remaining steps, and pulled open the glass door, which was much lighter than he had expected. It banged back on its hinges, but he was already through, Kir right behind him. The robot didn't know why they were running, but the partners worked together so closely that they moved as a unit.

The wide hallway Jones had gone down had a scattering of

people, standing and talking, or going from one doorway to the next. Jones was gone. Laughton went to the closest doorway, and looked in. A robot on a couch was plugged in to a charger, his system shut down.

Laughton's pulse seemed to fill his chest, running across his shoulder blades. They were still on the preserve, weren't they? What was a robot doing here?

"What is it?" Kir said behind him.

"A robot."

"No, the guy we were chasing?"

Laughton turned to Kir, raising his voice. "It's a goddamn robot," he said, pointing. "Are we still on the preserve? You said we were on the preserve."

Kir looked at the inert object sitting on the couch. "Shit," he said.

"You think? What's going on here?"

"But the guy we were chasing just now was human."

"That was Jones, the trafficker who I let go."

Kir scanned their surroundings. "Come on. He's over there."

Laughton could smell the room from several feet away. It showed a sign on the door, the silhouette of a man and a woman, separated by a line: the bathroom. It wouldn't take long for the john to acquire such a reek of nauseating proportions, just a day or two, but the plumbing to the place must have been off since the founding of the preserve, possibly before that if the place had already become a robot establishment. Nine months of human waste, even if it was only a few humans and for part of the time, could only be withstood by desperate people. As long as it wasn't raining, Laughton figured people went outside and used the lake out back whenever possible.

"I don't know if I can go in there," Laughton said.

Kir considered this, then understood. "It smells," he said. "Damn right it does."

"I'll get him." The robot put his hand to the door.

Laughton put a hand on his partner's shoulder. "Wait. The asshole can take his medicine. He won't last long in there."

They took up posts on either side of the door, their backs to the wall, as though they were bodyguards waiting for someone of importance to do his business. As they stood there, Laughton began to realize that many of what he had taken to be people when they came in were actually robots, recent models, no plastic old-timers, no anthropomorphized toasters. These were designer models with wheels, jewel-encrusted faces devoid of simul-skin, even one with electric jet thrusters, an enhancement so expensive that Laughton had never seen one in person. That same robot had three memory sticks plugged into exposed ports on the top of his head. Laughton just hoped he didn't fly when he was fucked up, although a metal piece of shit crashing out here wouldn't necessarily be a bad thing.

When he passed, Kir said, "Can you believe this shit?"

"Looks like the preserve might be the best thing that's ever happened out here. At least somebody's profiting."

"Metal pieces of shit," Kir said.

Laughton laughed at his partner echoing his own thoughts.

"Hey, I can say that," Kir said. "I'm a metal piece of shit too."

"Bleeding heart," Laughton said.

Kir held a finger up to his lips. His sensors picked up the movement just before the bathroom door opened. The wave of skank made Laughton gag and his eyes water. How the fuck had Jones stayed in there that long? Kir threw his arm across Jones's shoulder before the dealer even had a chance to register they'd been waiting for him.

"How did you stay in there for five minutes?" Laughton said.

Jones looked at Kir, who still had him in a tight grip as though he was a distant uncle overjoyed at seeing his little nephew all grown up. "You think you could ease up a little?"

Kir just grinned.

The dealer's eyes darted around them. He was still anxious as anything. Maybe not as agitated, but still panicked. That didn't make sense. If he'd hauled ass out here, wouldn't it be because it was a safe haven? Was he scared of Laughton, of the cops?

Two women went by with their arms around each other. The heavy skin under one of their eyes made her human. Laughton couldn't get a handle on what this place was.

Jones addressed Laughton. "You saw what was happening on the TV. The robots are coming."

"It seems you picked a place where the robots already are."

Jones's eyes wandered away. "Yeah, well I didn't realize K-B had let all of this mess in."

"K-B?" Laughton said. "Did you fucking say K-B?" Kawnac-B had been the number one supplier of human recreational drugs in Baltimore: heroin, mylos, juice, cocaine, all the ways people liked to waste their lives. It was lucrative, but Kawnac-B didn't do it for the money. He liked the power it gave him over the addicts. They were like his slaves, and whenever one of them turned up dead, which was often, the case ended up on Laughton and Kir's desk. It was always ruled an overdose—the addicts did it to themselves, didn't they?—but Laughton remained convinced that Kawnac-B took a more active role in helping those overdoses along.

"If you take an animal's food source, it's going to follow the food," Kir said.

"But these are robots here."

"Nah, there're more humans," Jones said.

"What the hell!" Laughton said.

"How many bodies we seen that pointed to Kawnac-B?" Kir said.

Laughton scoffed, falling into the routine. "Once a week."

"Twenty-seven," Kir said. "You see, I know that exactly."

Jones was trying to hold his head as far from the robot as possible.

"You know how hard it is to find twenty-seven humans in some places?" Kir said.

Jones seemed to be considering it, and then he pulled away from the robot, twisting his way out of the grip and then rubbing his shoulder. "Can we get away from this shit?" He nodded toward the bathroom.

It made Laughton realize that the pulsing under his eye wasn't the stress of the interview, but a nausea-induced head-ache. "Come on," he said. The three of them returned to the lobby. There was a clutch of upholstered armchairs toward the back of the room around a squat round table. They sat, Jones taking the seat that put his back to the wall. He seemed more comfortable, as though the little walk had given him a chance to collect himself, and figure out the situation.

"How'd you find me?" Jones said.

"In the shitter," Kir said.

"What's a robot cop doing on the preserve?" Jones said, addressing Laughton, and making a point of not looking at Kir.

Laughton held his hands out to either side to take in the whole club. "What's a robot drug joint doing on the preserve?" he said.

"I'm—" Jones started, and then cut himself off, wise

enough to know when saying nothing was better than trying to be right.

"This is Kir," Laughton said.

"Department of Health and Human Services," the robot added.

"He's here as a favor," Laughton said. "I'm trying to close this homicide, before Congress decides the preserve isn't really working out and Kir's bosses close it for us. This shit here doesn't make me feel like things are working out."

"You think people are going to stop getting high?" Jones said. "Of course K-B's going to come in!"

Preserve drug laws were more stringent than those in the outside robot world. The thinking had been that the druggies would just stay off the preserve, and if Laughton could count his blessings, it was that none of it had turned up in Liberty so far.

"What do you want from me?" Jones said.

"Believe it or not, we're not here for you. We came because we learned that sims were leaving the preserve out this way. Frankly, I'm surprised as hell you're here. I figured you'd disappeared into Charleston."

"Thought I'd be safer here. I'm of value to Kawnac-B."

"Kawnac-B's dealing sims now? I thought he stuck to human drugs."

"Drugs for humans, sims for robots, nobody knows he's out here. Import and export," Jones said.

"I thought you said the Sisters already had their trafficking chain."

"Look, I don't run anything like that. What do I know? K-B's under the radar, and has security."

"Sorry," Kir said. "This time tomorrow, this is a ghost town again."

Now Jones's eyes really went wide. "You can't do that," he said, his voice a mix of petulance and panic.

"Don't worry," Laughton said. "You're coming with us."

"*You can't protect me*," Jones said, almost beside himself again, like the first time.

eyebrows raised and pulled together, lower eyelids tense—genuine fear

"You hear the off-the-preserve news?" Kir said.

Jones looked down, turning his head away. "Those robot hot shots, right? I didn't have anything to do with that."

No one had said that he had. No one said it now.

The dealer huffed. "Fucking figures. You're not here because some orgo got done. Metals supremacist bastards. Heaven forbid some metals get deactivated."

Laughton couldn't help but agree. He knew Kir wasn't like that, that he really was here to try to prevent robot presence on the preserve, but any human knew that they were little better than chattel to some metals.

"I didn't have anything to do with those hot shots," Jones said. "Why would I kill my customers? How stupid is that?"

This was just a waste of time. It was like arguing with a child. Erica could get in moods like this, where she got focused on one thing in her mind, and wouldn't let go of it, ignoring everything that was being said that might have superseded whatever statement she'd latched on to, talking over them louder and louder. No one had accused Jones of anything. They'd hoped he'd give them a little information, and if he didn't want to come back with them, that was his problem. Kawnac-B would no doubt ensure that the body was never found.

Laughton stood up. "Let's find Kawnac-B," he said to Kir.

Jones sat up straight. "Wait, wait, what do you want to know?"

Laughton ignored him. "Come on," he said.

Kir stood too.

"Wait a second," Jones said, getting to his feet. "I'm sorry. See. I'm saying it. I'm sorry for running. I'll help however you need."

Laughton turned his back, and started across the lobby in the direction that Jones had been coming from when they'd arrived. He didn't look back to see what Jones was doing, but he suspected that the dealer would follow them, too nervous now to be on his own. He was probably working out what Kir had said about the place becoming a ghost town. Meant the authorities were probably on their way.

The opposite hallway was shorter than the one that contained the bathrooms. There were two lounges to either side, and then a bank of doors, the two center of which were open. Laughton and Kir went through the doors side by side. They were in an enormous dining room, round tables with white tablecloths, some intended for only two people, up to those that could seat ten. A large dance floor, in impeccable condition, defined one end of the room. The old-fashioned, very human space was like a time capsule of when humans were still the dominant life-form, and enough people would need to eat actual food to warrant a space of this size. Now there was a smattering of robots with a handful of humans spread out around the room.

"This has to be the most boring illegal club of all time," Laughton said.

"Just for your little orgo brain," Kir said.

Laughton saw the bar in the corner, a self-serve vending machine that showed a multicolored array of memory sticks through the glass. He looked back at the tables and saw that most of the robots were using, some so far gone that sticks were still in their ports. The party was in their cpu's. "We better get samples from the bar," he said. "Is the department on its way?"

"Hell, yeah. The department can come onto the preserve to clear out illegal robots, and come they will." Kir rolled his eyes. "Just got a message from Kawnac-B." He pointed to a window in the wall above them. It showed an expensive upstairs office with wood-paneled walls and a gilded ceiling. A tall stainless steel cylinder with a screen that wrapped around the top stood in the center of the window: Kawnac-B.

"I hate that robot," Laughton said.

"There are stairs over here," Kir said, heading toward the bar. Laughton followed.

"Hey," Jones called.

"You want to come?" Laughton said without stopping.

Jones hung back, and as the police reached the door to the stairs, Laughton saw Jones take a seat at one of the tables. Two identical robots got up from one of the other tables to go and join him. There was something familiar about them, but Laughton couldn't place what. He used his body cam to snap a picture, and then pushed it aside to focus on the meeting ahead.

When he and Kir had first come into contact with Kawnac-B years ago, the robot was still mostly humanoid. But as K-B toyed with people more and more, he found the idea of emulating such an easily destroyed machine beneath him. After modification after modification, he eventually settled on the cold metal cylinder as the ideal body. Like a Swiss Army knife, panels hid arms, blades, weapons, and more, each able to emerge instantaneously.

The door at the top of the stairs opened onto a little anteroom. Fake plants stood in bronze pots in the corners. Kir pulled the office door open, but before Laughton could go through, the robot shoved him, just as the springing sound of wires uncoiling registered in his mind: Taser.

Shaken, the chief rotated his shoulders and tried to sound unfazed as he stepped into the office, an opulent, wood-paneled room with an enormous rosewood desk, but no chairs. The large window that afforded a view of the ballroom made the space feel much larger than it was. A small elevator door was tucked into a corner. "Interesting choice, Kawnac-B."

The side of the screen nearest the police showed a CGI face in such high resolution that the only thing preventing it from looking real was that it was flat. "Just a little prank on old friends."

"So I'm sure you don't know that we're investigating a human murder in which the weapon was a Taser?"

"In Liberty?" the robot said, rolling on his three casters to the large desk in the center of the room. "Do you think I could make it to Liberty without being stopped? I'm surprised I lasted on the preserve this long. I assume I'm closing down tonight?"

"That may be negotiable," Kir said.

Negotiable? Laughton didn't know what Kir was doing, but he knew to keep quiet.

"I don't think you killed the human," Kir said. "But that doesn't mean you weren't involved."

"Dead humans, so of course *I'm* involved," Kawnac-B said, mocking them.

"See that guy down there?" Kir said, pointing at the window. Kawnac-B made no effort to look. "He's their distributor, and he's in your club, so yeah, you're involved."

"I don't know everyone who comes into my club."

"That why there are so many robots here? Robots usually aren't buying what you're selling."

"It sounds like you already have ideas," Kawnac-B said. "I'm just a club owner. Go ahead and take samples from the bar. Nothing illegal down there. Numbers mostly."

"Just heroin and meth and opioids. You always catered to the human population, after all."

"You really can't seem to decide what it is you want me for," Kawnac-B said.

Laughton hated the complete lack of body language in addition to the screen face. That was probably part of the point. "So how's it feel to have a boss?" Laughton said.

"Kind of pathetic, stuck in the backwoods," Kir said, picking up on Laughton's cue.

"Yeah, the Sisters really put a leash on you," Laughton said.

"I don't know what you're talking about." The robot's face and voice remained flat.

"How's it feel to be a pawn?" Laughton said.

"The two of you have decided something that has no basis in reality," Kawnac-B said.

"And what's that?" Laughton said.

"You tell me," Kawnac-B said.

Laughton took the maglock from his pocket, concealing it in his hand. "I'm running out of patience," he said, stepping forward.

"Why don't you just run *out*?" Kawnac-B said.

"You want us to leave, we want to leave," Laughton continued.

"Then leave."

Laughton shrugged, and then tossed the maglock. It attached itself to the robot's body with a smack.

Kawnac-B's face screen flickered, but he didn't comment on the fact that he had just been maglocked. He wasn't going to give them the satisfaction.

"This is bad business for your boss," Kir said. "Robots dying on sims just as you move into the field. Customers aren't going to keep buying if they think that each hit could be deadly."

"You better make sure that doesn't happen," Kawnac-B said.

"Was that a threat?"

"Did it sound like a threat? Get this thing off of me."

"Let's try this another way," Kir said. "If the people who deliver the perfectly legal numbers being sold in your perfectly illegal club left wanting something in exchange, might they leave with something that Sam and Smythe had a hand in?"

The face disappeared from the screen, leaving it black, and then it came back on, the whole thing lasting a second, a flicker. "Let's say, hypothetically, yes."

"Anything new coming out of here in the last few days?"

"Nothing new here in a week or so. Jones was supposed to show up with something, but he showed up with his tail between his legs, and nothing else."

"Says the metal who tried to kill me on sight," Laughton said.

"That had nothing to do with any of this. That's just because it was fun."

As they were talking, the room below them cleared out except for Jones, who continued to sit at the table, staring straight ahead. He must have warned everyone the party was over, or maybe Kawnac-B had sent out a message. They'd all be across the bridge and off the preserve before anyone from the Department of Health and Human Services would get here. With no arrests, they wouldn't clear them out for long, if not in this club, then somewhere else on the preserve with no people and little oversight.

"Come on, Kawnac-B," Kir said. "Give us something we can use. You really want the Sisters to run you?"

"I hate to disabuse you of anything, but I don't work with the Sisters. And you can believe me or not, but I had nothing to do with this."

"So who do you work with?"

It clicked for Jesse. Of course, Kawnac-B wasn't working with the Sisters. That's why Crisper noticed a new route, because a competitor was siphoning off the product. "Titanium," he said, shaking his head. "That's the new route." And that was why Jones was here, probably. He figured Smythe dead, Sam missing. Maybe time to look somewhere other than the Sisters. "The preserve opens," Laughton continued, "and as a dealer in orgo drugs, your clientele moves. You follow, importing the drugs in, which means you have a delivery network into the preserve, might as well transport things out on the way back. Did you come up with the name Titanium? It's got a nice ring to it."

"You are, again, way off base."

"*Way* off base?" Laughton said.

"I think maybe just a *little* off base," Kir said.

"I don't think I'm at all off base," Laughton said.

"I am not Titanium."

"What are you, stainless steel?"

"Very funny, meat man."

"Watch it," Kir said.

"No, it's okay," Laughton said. "If he's Titanium, I'm meat, I get it."

"I am *not* Titanium. I've never even met Titanium, or seen the guy."

"But you do know him," Laughton said.

"Of course he does," Kir said. "He's the one running our good friend K-B here."

"No one—"

But before Kawnac-B could finish, the elevator door

opened, and two enormous robots covered in black nonconducting bulletproof vests and helmets stepped into the room brandishing carbines. A squat robot in a black suit, no more than four feet tall, stood behind them. In comparison to the armed robots, he looked like a child.

At the sight of them, Kawnac-B's screens went black. He wasn't going to get involved.

"Mark Sysigns, Homeland Security," the robot in the suit said.

A movement in the room down below caught Laughton's eye. Two more robots in riot gear, the letters "HSI" in white on their backs. "Shit," he said. "Can I see some ID?"

"Oh, right," Sysigns said, pulling a badge from his pocket.

"He's legitimate," Kir said. They'd already exchanged credentials electronically.

Laughton checked the proffered ID anyway. It was for the Coast Guard Investigative Service. Sure, the Coast Guard was Homeland Security, but why would they be this far inland?

"I called in Department of Health and Human Services," Kir said to the Homeland Security man.

"We were closer," Sysigns said.

"If you're that close," Laughton said, "why has this club stayed open?" Laughton kept expecting to see more forces, but other than the three robots in the room, and the two down below, no other robots appeared. It seemed like a small team for such a raid.

"We're here now," Sysigns said. Realizing that wasn't really an answer, he said, "Jurisdiction."

"Nobody contacted me," Kir said.

One of the HSI men was removing Laughton's mag damper from Kawnac-B's silent figure. When it popped off, Kawnac-B's screen flickered on, showing nothing but a smiling mouth.

Laughton's muscles tensed with a desire to punch the robot in the face, crack his screen.

"We've got everything under control now," Sysigns said. "No need for you to stay."

"We can wait until the HHS arrives," Kir said.

"I called them off," the short robot said. "We've got this."

Laughton and Kir exchanged looks. Laughton could see that his partner was even more skeptical of this whole thing than he was. "Come on," Kir said.

"I want my maglock back," Laughton said, holding out his hand.

Sysigns took it from the agent, and held it out to Laughton.

"Elevator?" Laughton asked.

"Be my guest, gentlemen," Sysigns said, stepping out of the way.

The chief and Kir stepped forward.

"You're sure you don't need help?" Kir said.

"Most of the patrons here were on the run by the time we showed up. I've got men trailing them outside."

This whole thing felt wrong. It had felt wrong from the moment they'd pulled up to the club, but this was even worse. "Fine. Whatever," Laughton said. He entered the elevator, and Kir joined him. Once the door closed, the chief said, "What the hell?"

"They got here very quickly for Homeland Security," Kir said.

"Why am I starting to feel like the whole preserve is a sham?"

"It's not a sham, but Homeland Security's anti-sims policy might be based on this bullshit."

"At least we found Jones," Laughton said.

"Yeah," Kir said, but he was thinking, his mind somewhere

else. Or maybe he was actually conversing with someone in his department silently.

Laughton wondered how he had been so unaware of what was happening on and around the preserve. Maybe Liberty was a way of putting his head in the sand, and he was fooling himself to think he was doing anything of importance. It seemed like there were many greater forces involved.

"Let's get Jones and get the hell out of here," Laughton said as the elevator door opened into a room adjacent to the larger dining room.

"Hell yeah," Kir said.

But when they returned to the dining room, it was empty. Jones was gone.

It was a little after 2:00 a.m. when Laughton's truck pulled into his driveway. The plucky GPS announced, "You have arrived." Laughton was awake, but his face hurt and he needed the day to be over. Tossing the maglock, the weight leaving his hand, and then the satisfying snap as it attached itself to that metal bastard . . . that had felt good. A million times better than playing limousine service to a bunch of drunks. But the bad taste of their run-in with Homeland Security soured an already terrible evening. And Jones was in the wind again.

Inside, Laughton used the flashlight on his phone rather than turning on the lights. "There's a charger cord in the corner," he said, shining the light in that direction. "We're one hundred percent solar, so I don't know how strong a charge you're going to get."

"It's fine," Kir said.

"You need anything else?"

"Go to sleep," Kir said. "You need the rest more than I do."

But Laughton wavered. He felt the pull of the bed upstairs, but he didn't want to leave Kir either. It wasn't that he had something to say to him. He just wanted the companionship, the comfort, feeling like himself in a way he hadn't realized he didn't anymore. "I missed you," he said at last.

"You wouldn't believe . . ." Kir said.

"Okay. Good night."

"Jesse, we're going to get them," Kir said. "We always do."

"Selective memory," Laughton said.

"Robots can't have selective memories."

"Right," Laughton said, laying some heavy irony in his voice. He turned and went upstairs. Halfway up, he could hear the charging cord unspool from the wall socket.

On the landing, he considered Erica's door. It was closed, but not latched, the cool glow of her nightlight just visible between the door and the jamb. She liked to have it closed enough to block out any noise that he or Betty might make before they turned in, but having it latched made her anxious, so this was her compromise. He peeked through the crack, but it was too dark to make her out. He was afraid if he went in, he would wake her, so he turned to the bathroom instead. He propped his phone on the edge of the sink so that the flashlight was shining on the floor, giving enough light to see by, but not so much as to hurt his eyes.

He used the toilet, thankful for the Liberty waterworks that prevented the horror of the bathroom out in Santee. He counted the hours before he needed to be up again, and it was too short. He flicked off the light on his phone, and went into the bedroom. Betty rolled over on the bed, her shape a black outline in the darkness. Her voice, coated in sleep, came out with a sigh. "Hey."

"Hey," he whispered. "You're supposed to be asleep."

"How was your thing?"

"Fine. We'll talk in the morning."

"No, I'm up, I'm up," she said, slurring her words together. "Come." And he could see the silhouette of her outstretched arms. He pulled off his shoes, slid the shirt over his head, undid his belt, and stepped out of his pants, climbing into bed in just his boxers and socks. He lay on his back as Betty scooted herself over to him, rolling so her head was on his chest, her body wedged against him. Every muscle in Laughton's body relaxed.

He felt himself sinking into the mattress. He closed his eyes, his face tingling.

"Kir plugged in downstairs?"

"Yeah."

"So much for taking it easy," Betty said.

"Taking it easy" was why Laughton had come to Liberty. The thinking had been that the stress and hours of city homicide made his facial pain and headaches worse. After nine months, he wasn't sure either was any better, but he'd been available to Betty and Erica more, and that was a win, if nothing else. "Hon?" he said, but Betty was already asleep again.

He squeezed her. After a moment, she rolled away from him, and then he turned onto his side, and lay there, so exhausted he couldn't sleep. He remembered his phone, and leaned over the edge of the bed to hook his pants with his finger and retrieved the phone from the pocket. He placed it on the charger on his bedside table, and dropped back onto his pillow.

His mind slid into Kawnac-B's club even as he tried to suppress the thought, to clear his head. Crisper's map had proven accurate, and that meant they'd have to check out the harbor to figure out how sims were leaving by boat. It also confirmed that Titanium was not a myth. If it turned out this whole thing came down to a turf war . . . He needed to find the Sisters. But there was that stupid meeting at Charleston police headquarters in the morning. Damn it!

He flopped over on his other side, and closed his eyes. He just needed sleep. If only he could will his body to shut down.

In the morning, when Laughton took his phone off the charger, he was greeted with the headline "Nine More Robots Burned." The words made his throat close up. The situation was devolving faster than he could handle it. The fact that the article didn't link the deadly virus to the preserve yet was only a small consolation. He jumped out of bed and put on the same clothes he had been wearing the day before.

Kir was fixing eggs for Erica in the kitchen, and Betty's mom was at the table, the lower half of her face swollen, purple and yellow. She mumbled, "Good morning," through clenched teeth.

"Morning," he said, and then to Kir, "Did you see the news?"

"Yes."

"Any word from your boss?"

" 'Hurry up,' " Kir said.

"Then she shouldn't have us scheduled for meetings in eff-ing Charleston. Let's go."

Betty came up behind him. "Aren't you eating something?"

Laughton kissed her on the top of the head. "No time," he said. "Be good for mom and grandma," Laughton called to Erica. Then he and Kir left.

In the truck, on the way to the meeting where Laughton and Kir would have to convince the army, Homeland Security, and the FBI that Smythe's murder was not a valid reason to seize the preserve from the Department of Health and Human Services, Laughton kneaded his forehead with the bases of his palms, and grunted.

"What is it?" Kir said.

Laughton shook his head, as though to clear it. "Nothing," he said.

Kir nodded without saying anything, and Laughton was grateful again to have his partner, someone who knew when to lend silent support. In the quiet, he tried to get a picture of the whole case in his mind. The orgo drug trade and the robot drug trade were intertwined, and the preserve, with its legal status outside of the robotic purview—at least for now—was the hub.

The Sisters, who had already run the sims trade in the south-east, had dominated the business since the preserve opened, but a new player, Titanium, was moving in. Carl Smythe and Sam McCardy had been two of the best sims programmers on the preserve, and their product was moved through Jones by the Sisters. Smythe was murdered, and McCardy and Jones both disappeared at the same time that a deadly virus started killing robot addicts. How did it all fit with the murder? Any one of these things could be relevant, or none of them could be. Perhaps they had gotten too far away from the actual murder. They needed to step away from all of the noise.

He pulled out his phone, and opened the photos he had taken of the crime scene. The body slumped against the back of the grocery store, its chin resting on its chest. The slashed-open arm and leg were perhaps most arresting for the lack of blood. It looked like such a severe trauma, but impossibly clean. Laughton zoomed in on the arm. There was no way to see the hidden pouch that Dr. Conroy had found. He pulled the image around, trying to focus on the ground around the body, instead of the corpse itself, but there was nothing but weather-beaten asphalt, pebbles, and grime.

"You find something?" Kir said.

"Just going back over everything." Laughton swiped to the next photo. It was a wider shot of the back of the building: the delivery truck, the police cruiser, several people standing around. He zoomed in to look at each of the people that he had talked to that day, trying to read their expressions.

Larry Richman and the kid Ryan had almost the same expression—

lips tight and drawn back toward the ears, eyebrows pulled together—anxious bordering on fear

The produce deliveryman stood separate from the others,

but his face bore almost the same expression. Laughton remembered that micro-expression that had flashed across the driver's face when he'd asked him if he knew Smythe. What was the guy's name? Laughton minimized the photo and tapped his notepad, scrolling back up to the top. Barry Slattery.

Laughton jumped back to the photograph. The program had automatically returned it to its usual size, showing the whole scene. Laughton began to zoom back in on Barry, when he noticed the truck behind the driver. The lettering on the side— "Shit," he said.

"What?" Kir said.

"I'm so stupid," Laughton said. The lettering on the side of the truck, above the hand-painted picture of the cornucopia, said "Sisters." "Look." He held the phone so Kir could see.

"What?"

"The truck. It says 'Sisters.' I knew that guy was hiding something when I talked to him, but I was too distracted to push it." He turned the phone back so he could get into the police database, and searched for Barry Slattery. "The Sisters use their produce business to transport their sims. One of their men just happens to be at the crime scene? I thought he was nervous just because who wouldn't be? He didn't seem worse than that."

The database had returned an address for Slattery, and Jesse leaned forward to input it on the GPS's touch screen.

"This bastard better be home," Laughton said.

"We better let Commissioner Ontero and Secretary Pattermann know we're going to be late," Kir said.

"Fuck them," Laughton said.

"I'll stick with we're going to be late." The robot sent the message.

This stretch of road was becoming familiar to the chief. The mixed vegetation, fields, then woods, then fields, didn't seem quite as wild as it had a few days ago. Now it was simply the corridor to civilization.

The commissioner's name popped up on the dashboard screen. He'd gotten the message they were going to be late. Laughton opened up the line. "What the hell, Jesse. I told you, you needed to be here for this meeting. I *need* you to be here for this meeting."

"We've got a lead. We need to bring him in while we can."

"Who?"

Jesse felt an overwhelming reluctance to say. He wasn't quite sure why. "I don't want to jump the gun," Laughton said.

"Damn it, Jesse, what did I say about professional courtesy?"

"Look, if you know, the metals are going to try to pull it out of you. It's better that you can answer truthfully you don't know."

"Or you could tell me and I can send out some cars."

"Can't risk scaring him off," Laughton said, not trusting anyone else to make the approach. "This guy knows me." And would be just as likely to run at the sight of Laughton, if he had anything to hide, but this was the chief's case and he didn't want other people working it.

There was a pause while the commissioner thought. "Okay," he said at last, resolve bolstering his voice. "Go get him and I'll cover here as long as I can."

"Right," Laughton said.

"Good break," the commissioner said.

"About fucking time," Laughton said.

"You said it, not me." And he hung up.

Laughton didn't envy Ontero his job. He looked at the arrival time estimate on the GPS. Fifteen minutes. Come on, Barry. Be there.

Barry lived about a mile west of the Ashley River. Laughton didn't know the name of the neighborhood. The roads were narrow, just wide enough to maybe allow two cars to get past one another. The weedy lawns gave way to sandy dirt at the edge of the street where cars had driven onto people's yards to avoid collisions. The houses were glorified shacks, probably called cottages by real estate agents when they were built—one story, maybe twenty feet wide with a door and a single window in the front. They were only a driveway's width apart. Some indeterminate green growth coated the lower half of most of the houses, making them look rundown and shabby. They passed a single well-tended lawn being cared for by a gardening bot, a low-order robot classed as a machine with no artificial intelligence, and therefore legal on the preserve. Barry's house was two away from where the gardener was working. The awning over the front door was tilted, pulling away from the house on one side.

The chief pulled into the empty driveway, hoping the driveway was empty because Barry didn't have a car, not that he had already taken off.

"Anyone in there?" the chief said to Kir.

The robot, using his infrared vision, nodded. "Someone is."

"Just one?"

Kir shook his head. "Two."

"Okay," he said, and he got out of the truck.

The front door opened, revealing Barry in red basketball

shorts that fell below his knees and a T-shirt with the sleeves cut off. Before he could say anything, the slap of a screen door slamming out back shot through the quiet. Barry turned and yelled into the house, "Sam!" Kir had already vaulted onto the roof in a rare display of his engineered prowess, running across the top of the house toward the back.

Laughton, pulling out his gun, pushed past Barry into the house, rushed through the living room without even registering his surroundings, into the kitchen, then plunged into a weed-tangled backyard. Kir, jumping from the roof, landed in the alley in front of him and started running after a motorbike that disappeared between two of the other houses, its motor grinding like a buzz saw.

Kir followed, but Laughton stayed behind, lowering his weapon, knowing he couldn't hope to make any progress on foot. He could hold on to Barry at least, prevent the young man from following his friend's lead. But the genial vegetable deliveryman was standing just inside the screen door at the back of the house, watching. "Who was that?" Laughton said, opening the door.

Barry stepped back as Laughton let himself in. "Nobody."

eyes avoiding the chief's face, lips thin, lower eyelids barely visible—lying and afraid

Laughton stepped toward the man, and Barry stepped back, pressed against the kitchen wall. Laughton was in his face. "I don't have time for you to lie to me. And don't think you'll get away with it this time."

"This time! Ah, man, what are you talking—"

"Who was that who just flew out of here?"

"He'd just come in late last night, like middle of the night."

"Who!"

"Man, I don't want any part of this," Barry said, turning his head down and away, holding his hands up in front of him.

"It's too late for that."

They both turned to look as the screen door opened, and Kir appeared. The robot shook his head, one short movement.

Laughton put his face uncomfortably close to the deliveryman's. "Who was that?"

"I swear, I didn't know that was who you were after, or I would have called."

Laughton put both his hands flat against the wall to either side of Barry's head, boxing the man in.

"It was Sam," Barry said. "Sam McCardy."

Laughton dropped his hands and took a step back. McCardy? He'd hoped maybe it was Jones, who had clearly ditched his original car, since GPS showed it sitting in place out in Santee, still at the drug club.

"He say where he was going?" Kir said.

Barry's shoulders dropped in relief. He must have figured if they were going to arrest him, they'd have done it already. He shook his head. "I really don't know."

no micro-expressions—he's telling the truth

"Could you make a guess?" Laughton said.

Eyes widening for a moment, shaking his head, he said, "I don't know. The Sisters?"

"But he came to you first," Kir said.

"Could you give me a little more space," Barry said to Laughton. "You're making me nervous here."

"Maybe we should sit down," Kir said as Laughton stepped back. "We're not here to arrest you. We just need your help."

Laughton wasn't so sure they weren't going to arrest the guy—being at the scene of the crime made him a suspect—but he knew Kir was trying to make him comfortable. The last thing they needed was for Barry to suddenly decide he wouldn't talk until he saw a lawyer.

"Yeah," Barry said, nodding. "Yeah, sure, okay." He stepped past Laughton. "Can I get either of you anything? A drink?"

"No, thank you," Kir said.

Laughton tapped his wrist at his partner. They were short on time.

"Maybe in here?" Kir said.

Barry nodded like he just remembered that he had another room in the house. He led the way into the living room. There were two puffy, leather couches facing one another, worn tan where people had sat on them over the years. A projector sat on the metal-and-glass coffee table between the couches, pointed at the blank space above a defunct fireplace.

"You live here alone?" Laughton said as he and Kir sat down on the couch opposite the one Barry had selected.

"This was actually my grandma's house, way back," Barry said.

"You grew up in Charleston?"

"Only in summers," Barry said.

Laughton nodded. The memory had relaxed Barry further. Laughton didn't want to risk losing that. "It's a nice city," he said. "We lucked out when the government decided to locate the preserve here."

"That we did."

"Did you know," Laughton said, "that robots from various branches of the government are on the preserve right now, arguing that this murder . . ."

lower eyelid shrinking—rising anxiety

". . . proves humans shouldn't be allowed to govern and police themselves."

"I saw something of that on TV."

"I'm just trying to prove them wrong," Laughton said.

Barry looked from Laughton to Kir, and Kir to Laughton. "I don't know how I can help you."

"First, and I hate to have to do this, but you were at the scene of the crime and work for the Sisters . . ."

"I didn't kill Carl."

Laughton held out a hand. "All right, I had to ask."

"I didn't."

no flicker in expression—most likely the truth

"You'll have to understand if I'm a little skeptical of what you say, because let's go back to what you told me at the crime scene. You said you didn't recognize Carl Smythe, but seeing as it was Sam McCardy that just rabbited out of here, I kind of don't think that's the truth."

"I didn't recognize him," Barry said, "because I'd never seen him before, but I heard you guys mention his name, and well, Sam and I *were* friends—are friends," he corrected himself. "We trade ROM files online for old video games."

Laughton remembered all of the old video game consoles in McCardy's place, now melted and destroyed. "He didn't come here last night to play video games," Laughton said. He waited for Barry to speak. After a minute he said, "So he got here last night . . ."

Barry nodded. "It was like midnight, I guess," he said.

Laughton sought to prod him some more. "He was looking for a place to stay?"

"What he— Yeah."

"He wanted something else too," Laughton said.

"He's scared out of his mind," Barry said. "He wasn't really making sense. He wanted me to introduce him to the Sisters. Said they were going to kill him otherwise."

Kir said, "Because they'd killed Smythe? Is that why?"

Barry shook his head. "Naw. No. You think the Sisters killed Smythe?"

"Do you?"

He wiped his lips with his hand, and shook his head. "Naw."

"You work for the Sisters," Kir said.

"I run deliveries—legitimate deliveries," he hurried to add.

"They run a vegetable farm," Laughton said.

"Most of the produce in the state comes from their farm," Barry said.

"But you also deliver sims and drugs."

Barry shook his head. "Never drugs. Never people drugs."

"But sims," Laughton said.

"I didn't say that."

"How long have you been working for the Sisters?"

"Two years."

So before the preserve. "Do you think the Sisters would kill a hacker who was causing them trouble?"

Barry's eyes darted between them, a slight panic. "I wouldn't know."

"But Sam thought they would."

"I couldn't say. All I know, he came because he wanted me to introduce him to them. He said he'd screwed something up, and he had a really good deal for them if they would protect him."

"From who?" Kir said.

Barry shook his head. "He wouldn't say." His expression remained consistent. He was telling the truth.

"So his best friend was killed. He's worried someone's going to kill him too. What did he have to offer the Sisters? A sim?"

"I don't think so."

"Don't think?"

"He didn't say, but I think . . ." He took a deep breath. "I'm just the delivery guy," he said. "Don't shoot the messenger, right?"

Laughton and Kir both stayed silent.

Barry watched them, waiting for reassurance. When none came, he sighed, and said, "I think he meant that he had the antivirus for this thing that's killing robots."

Laughton felt his stomach drop down into his bowels. It was possible there *was* an antivirus and it hadn't burned up in the hackers' house?

"Why do you say that?" Kir said.

"He had a memory stick in his pocket, and he kept pulling it out, like he was making sure it was still there. I guess it could be a sim, but it just, he kept saying it was worth more than just money. They'd want it because it would be leverage."

Laughton nodded. It was still just as likely a sim, but Barry's theory made sense. "But he was afraid if he went to them directly, they'd kill him?"

"Yeah," Barry said.

Laughton tried to figure this. When the hacker ran at first, it was clearly with something else in mind. Jones had been making inroads with Titanium. Maybe McCardy thought that was what he needed to do too. But something changed that? Or he'd gone somewhere else? "Did he say where he'd been hiding?" Laughton said.

Barry shook his head. "No."

"What else did he say?"

"Nothing," Barry said. "He crashed soon after he got here. Woke up like twenty minutes before you showed up. Then he was just eager to meet the Sisters."

So, Sam and Smythe release the virus together, Laughton thought. *They then can sell the antivirus for huge money to the sims traders, to preserve their client base and reputation. When Smythe gets killed, however, McCardy panics. Doesn't know who to trust. So he comes to his gamer buddy who has connections.* "One thing that's bothering me," Laughton said, "is that you were at the crime scene. If the Sisters were going to kill Sam and Smythe, having one of their men there seems like a huge coincidence."

"You think I haven't thought that?" Barry said. "It's driving me crazy."

"You've got an explanation?" Kir said.

"I don't know. Look, if they were trying to get to the Sisters around Jones, then maybe Carl came to meet me for that purpose, and someone killed him before I got there."

"What do you think?" Laughton said to Kir. This was one of their old routines, to discuss something openly in front of an interviewee as a way of playing their anxieties.

"Makes sense to me," Kir said.

"But we should still bring him in, just in case, while we go check things out."

"Whoa," Barry said. "No need to bring me in. I'm not going to rabbit, I swear."

The partners both turned toward him.

"Is he telling the truth, Jesse?" Kir said.

"Tell us where we can find the Sisters," Laughton said.

"Ah, man," Barry said.

"Did you tell McCardy where to find them?"

Barry shook his head very fast. "No."

"Okay," Laughton said. "Tell us where *we* can find them, and I think I'll trust you to be where we can find you when we need you."

Barry sighed, his shoulders dropping, and his eyes opening up. "I don't know if there's any address. There are no numbers around in there."

"Show me," Laughton said, holding out his phone, open to the maps app. Without letting go, he allowed Barry to move the map around until he pointed to a building. Laughton dropped a digital pin into it. "Let me give you my info so you can call me if he comes back." Barry fished his phone out of his pocket, and they tapped phones. "One more thing," Laughton said. "You think McCardy did this? Maybe he and Carl got into a fight?"

Barry shook his head. "I really don't know. All I know, he was panicked."

"Don't you panic now," Laughton said.

Barry shook his head, but his eyebrows were knit in fear.

"Worst thing you could do would be to disappear."

Barry nodded.

"Jesse," Kir said with the polite sternness that said he had something that couldn't wait and couldn't be said in public, but before Laughton could respond, a text came through on his phone, and then it began to buzz almost immediately thereafter. He pulled it out, and his eyebrows frowned, the commissioner's office. Barry's cell was ringing now too. What happened?

"All our friends from Washington just hit the news," Kir said as Laughton accepted the call. His stomach felt as though it had been pulled through his feet. "Laughton," he said.

The commissioner's secretary said, "One moment," and then the commissioner was on. "Chief Laughton, I need you to come in now, please. The federal authorities are not happy about the delay. They want to speak with the man in charge of the homicide." His tone was chummy, but stilted. He was not alone.

The sound of another text coming in. Barry rushed into the kitchen, talking breathlessly on the phone.

"Um," Laughton stalled. "I'm onto something."

"When can you be here?" the commissioner said with a big smile in his voice.

Laughton was eager to get to the Sisters. Knowing that McCardy was looking to make contact with them, he wanted to get there first. "Say at least an hour. Tell them I'm all the way on the other side of the preserve." He knew they'd be too busy to bother to GPS his phone.

"Two hours?" the commissioner said, trying to buy him extra time. Laughton felt an unusual surge of warmth toward the man. "We'll see you— What?" the commissioner said to someone who was with him. His voice grew even more pinched. "It's got to be now," the commissioner said to Laughton, "twenty minutes."

Shit, Laughton thought. *Shit, shit, shit.* "Then I need immediate surveillance on two locations."

"Send them to me."

"Okay," he said.

The commissioner hung up.

Chief Laughton looked at the texts he'd received, both from Betty. The first, "They're coming!" and the second, "You promised!" And then a third came through right then. "Get back here now." This was followed with a series of emoji, crying, screaming, fuming. If he didn't call her, she'd have a heart attack.

"Betty?" Kir said.

He nodded, texting the commissioner Barry's address and the location Barry had given them for the Sisters' home base. Then he called Betty. She picked up before it had even rung once. "I knew it. I knew they'd never let us alone. They just wanted to get us all in one place so it was easier to wipe us out."

"Betty . . ."

"Don't tell me I'm overreacting. You know your history."

"Okay," he said. The panic in Betty's voice was frightening. He didn't know what she would do, and he couldn't get to her, and now he had this meeting with the very robots freaking her out. If he told her that, she'd think he was going to be killed.

"You need to make this better," she said.

"I'm trying."

"No, you need to come here, and make this better."

"Betty, they're not taking over the preserve. They've got to look into the sims connections to these robot deaths, and that happens to be on the preserve. They're here as guests." He heard himself giving the official spiel without even having been briefed, and it made him sick. Is this how it happens? We all just keep fooling ourselves until it's too late? "Listen, I just got a big break. I need to work on this, and I might be able to get the feds to leave before they send more robots in."

"Are you just saying that?" Betty said.

"No," he said, hoping it sounded true. The click of a call waiting came through. He pulled the phone away from his ear to see who it was. His mother.

Bringing the phone back to his ear, he heard Betty reply with a small "Okay."

"Let me go," he said.

"Promise me," Betty said.

"I promise," he said without either of them detailing exactly what the promise was. He hung up, switching to his mother. "Mom, I can't talk right now."

"But you're okay? The news says there are robots on the preserve. They're going to shut it down?"

"Mom."

"What's happening?"

"Mom!"

"A mother gets to worry about her son."

"Don't I know it."

"How's Erica?"

"She's with her mother. Call them. I really need to go."

"Be safe," she said. "I love you."

"Take care."

"Bye-bye."

He hung up. The two calls back-to-back left him feeling drained and off balance.

"Ready?" Kir said, thankfully not prying.

Laughton nodded. He went over to the door frame leading into the kitchen. Barry was talking into his phone with his free hand pressed against his forehead, like he needed to hold his head in place. "We're going," he said to Barry.

"Good," Barry said without taking the phone away from his mouth. "'Cause I'm done. I'm just done."

Laughton watched the frazzled young man, and it made him feel helpless. He turned and walked away.

In the truck they had the radio tuned to the Charleston PD. There was a lot of chatter about the metals moving in, a lot of things said that shouldn't have been said on an open channel. He'd never tolerate that kind of unnecessary traffic on the radio from his officers, but everyone was in a panic. People were talking about rumors of a blockade in the harbor. Just the idea made Laughton's throat squeeze tight, and he brought both hands to his forehead, rubbing the top of his head in panic.

Kir turned off the radio. "They won't have any kind of real blockade in place until tomorrow," he said.

"You guessing?"

"I'm listening," he said, indicating that part of his system was taking updates from official channels. "Narcotics and the Coast Guard. Not us." Laughton's face must have appeared stricken, because Kir said, "I know. But I swear I'll protect the preserve."

"Just like I promised Betty you metal bastards would stay off our land?"

Kir said nothing, and Laughton felt guilty immediately for having grouped his friend, using the slur. "Look," he said, "we'll hit the Sisters. Sounds like Sam's running from Titanium. Who would know better than the enemy?"

"Keep following the distribution line," Kir said.

"Won't end your robot deaths."

"If we kill the supply and pick up some scapegoats, I promise you I will get robot forces off the preserve. I *promise*."

"Yeah. Okay. First let's catch a killer."

"That's our job."

Laughton turned the radio on, but it was more of the same ignorant, fear bullshit from before, so he turned it off. No one was calling anything real in right now.

The robot agents had taken over a conference room as their command center. An officer led the way for Laughton and Kir. The officer—he couldn't have been more than twenty-three years old—kept glancing at Kir out of the corner of his eye. He must have figured that the robot was part of the team that had invaded headquarters, and it clearly made him nervous, his body too rigid, the muscles at the edges of his upper lip dimpling with the effort of suppressing a frown. Seeing the young man's fear made Laughton angry: angry that the metals were there, angry that nothing ever got better.

When they opened the door to the conference room, Laughton was overwhelmed by the number of robots present, but before he could even assimilate just how many there were, the commissioner had him by the shoulder, and was pulling him back into the hall, shutting the door behind him. The commissioner took one look at Kir, and then turned his attention to Chief Laughton. They all knew each other from pre-preserve days; the commissioner knew Kir could be trusted. "Tell me you have something that's going to help in there."

Laughton thought about the likelihood McCardy had the antivirus, and the chance they would find him. Instead, he said, "Is there anything that could help in there?"

"Besides a lightning storm? No," and to Kir, "Sorry."

Kir wasn't bothered by the suggestion that all his colleagues should be fried.

"We closed up Kawnac-B's club out west," Laughton said. "That's got to count for something."

"Let's hope so," the commissioner said. He suddenly looked very old. "Have you seen the news?"

"I think we're making the news," Laughton said.

The commissioner shook his head, pulling out his phone. "It's not all bad," he said, handing the phone over.

A video showed the mall in Washington. There was a large gathering of robots, some still humanoid in appearance, but many with nonbiological designs, too tall, or too small, exposed metal and plastic, synthetic hair, even hovering like a quadcopter off the ground. They were holding up signs, "Preserve the Preserve" and "Be Better Than Humans. Keep Our Promises."

"Is this going out over Preserve news?" Laughton said.

"I don't know. The important thing is that there's still tremendous robot support for the preserve," the commissioner said. "Those bots in there have to tread lightly, so let's give them something to hold them off." He opened the door to the conference room, and the three of them went in.

The room was the dingy room to be expected in any good police station. A ten-foot table, scarred on its surface by the graffiti of some bored officer, was too large for the room, making the space feel uncomfortably narrow and long. A mound of discarded printers, monitors, and ancient desktop computers filled one corner. The walls were dominated by several SMART Boards, one projecting a map of Charleston, another filled with dry-erase notes from some past briefing, a variety of names, dates, and locations. The bit of wall visible in the space between the boards was scuffed, gray marks all over the once-white paint.

Grace Pattermann, the sole human in the room, sat at the head of the conference table, a tablet and a phone faceup before her. Both screens flickered with movement, which the secretary ignored. Six robots stood around the table divided into pairs. Colonel Brandis was joined by another seven-foot army robot. The Mark Sysigns they'd run into at Kawnac-B's club stood beside another four-foot-tall robot, human in appearance aside from his size, who wore a white sailor's uniform. The final two robots, a man and a woman, wore the traditional black suits of the FBI. All sported robotic nonexpressions on their faces.

Chief Laughton felt Brandis's eyes on him. Just being in the room with the robot made Laughton nauseous.

"Kir," Grace Pattermann said.

Kir simply nodded as he positioned himself at the opposite end of the table, neither on the robots' side nor the humans'.

There was an awkward delay, no one sure who had the authority to start. Of course, there was no way for Laughton to tell if the robots weren't messaging each other silently. It was generally seen as rude to do so when two robots were in the same location, but Laughton always felt as though they were doing it anyway, having a conversation over his head like parents spelling things out in front of kids who can't read.

The commissioner tried to take charge. "This is Chief Jesse Laughton," he said. "He's chief of police in Liberty, one of our western settlements. He's heading the Smythe murder investigation."

"We know," Brandis said.

"We actually met last night," Mark Sysigns jumped in, revealing some kind of interdepartmental rivalry.

"Chief Laughton, we're eager to hear your report," the short robot said. "We understand your record in the Human Crimes Division of the Baltimore Police Department was astounding, so we expect great progress."

"'Astounding' seems a bit strong," Laughton said, but Kir

spoke over him, "Perhaps you'd care to introduce yourselves before you start interrogating a fellow law officer?"

"Perhaps the Department of Health and Human Services officer would like to make the introductions for us," Brandis said. "It's your job to be a liaison between the upper and lower orders."

"Peoples, Colonel," Kir said.

"I was being generous," the colonel said.

"Comparing humans to rudimentary AIs is hardly generous."

"You're right," the colonel said, and his tone made it clear that he wouldn't even consider a human on par with the lowest-order robot.

Laughton's face burned. He felt like a child who'd been caught doing something wrong, and was now helpless to the consequences.

Kir allowed disgust into his voice as he turned to Laughton and the commissioner. "Jesse," he said, "this is Colonel Brandis, army, and Lieutenant Cray. At the end of the table is—"

The robot who had said they were eager for the police's report interrupted, "Captain Sysigns," he said, "Coast Guard."

"Agents Asimov and Spectra, FBI," the woman in the suit said.

There were four branches of the robot government in the room. Laughton felt sick to his stomach at such a display of power. He tried to focus on the robot protest the commissioner had just shown him, because he'd promised Betty that this was not the end of the preserve, but in this room it felt a lot like it was.

"I've been assisting Chief Laughton personally since yesterday," Kir said, trying to draw everyone's attention, to protect Laughton and the commissioner. "We helped Mark Sysigns clean up a little mess on preserve lands last night."

"We're data mining as we speak," Mark Sysigns said.

"Much easier to do when you have the perps in hand," Kir said. "Chief Laughton was rather outraged that Homeland Security is so unconcerned with upholding the legal boundaries of the preserve, and frankly I was appalled."

"It's not Homeland Security's job to police the preserve," Sysigns said. "In fact, we're expressly forbidden to."

Colonel Brandis jumped in, recognizing that Homeland Security had allowed themselves to be on the defensive and shifting the briefing back in the intended direction. "If Chief Laughton is such an outstanding policeman, then he can tell us what he's doing about policing the humans who are murdering each other and attacking robots from the safety of the preserve."

"There's no evidence that there have been any attacks from the preserve," the commissioner said, unable to hold back his anger.

"We actually have very good evidence that Killer Apps originated here," Brandis said.

"Killer Apps?" Laughton said.

"That's what they're calling the virus," Mark Sysigns said.

"In fact," Brandis continued, "digital markers left in the victims suggest very strongly that Killer Apps is a Sam and Smythe program, and Kir of the HHS is very aware of that intelligence." He directed the end of that at Kir.

"And *we* think it was robots who killed Sam and Smythe," Kir said. "No doubt after they did the work for robot terrorists."

"Nobody's claiming anything about terrorists," Sysigns said.

Laughton watched the robots argue, relieved that they seemed to have forgotten him.

Grace Pattermann said, "The president has no doubts that this is a human attack launched from the perceived safety of the preserve, exactly the kind of unlawfulness that people

feared when the preserve was being debated by the last administration."

"And I have no doubt that this is a robot-led attack meant
to undermine public support for the preserve," Kir said. "Perhaps not even a private attack."

The accusation hung over everything for a moment.

Colonel Brandis said, "We're not here to debate politics.
Now, I'm prepared to set up a cordon, and the Coast Guard
has already begun to set up a blockade—"

"We're moving ships into position," Captain Sysigns said.
"We need perhaps twenty-four hours."

"Like a physical barrier matters to a computer program,"
Kir said. "A program that's already off-preserve! This is just
the president's excuse to turn the preserve into the prison he
wants. Are there trucks with rolls of wire fences waiting out on
the highway?"

"Kir. Enough," Grace Pattermann said, silencing the room.

Agent Spectra focused her attention on Chief Laughton
and said, "Well, maybe Chief Laughton can give us a reason
to not take such drastic measures. Isn't that the purpose of this
meeting?"

Everyone turned to the chief. Laughton had to resist the
feeling in the back of his throat that he had to retch. He tried
to get a signal from Kir, but he couldn't read any advice in his
partner's face. "I understand that you've lost an alarming number of robots in a short period of time," he said. "We're doing
our best—"

"No," Colonel Brandis said. "What are you doing?"

Kir said, "We're solving a murder."

Brandis ignored him, keeping his eyes on Laughton.

"We believe Smythe was murdered because he had the
antivirus."

"Because they'd *written* the virus," Colonel Brandis said. "These men were radical orgo terrorists."

Grace Pattermann said, "There've been no terrorist claims—"

"I don't need a claim to know what terrorism is," Brandis said.

"We'll leave that to you," Laughton said, surprising himself by his impertinence. "All I can say is that we think Smythe had the antivirus, and we're pretty sure that McCardy has it now."

"Good," Agent Asimov said. "Tell us what you've got, and we'll track these orgos down."

"Not on the preserve you won't," Grace Pattermann said. "You're here as guests of the preserve only."

"It's in everyone's best interest to have as many people working on this as possible," Agent Spectra said.

"You work on containing on your end. The commissioner and Chief Laughton with Kir as the HHS representative will take care of the preserve. This meeting is a courtesy."

"We'll see how long that lasts," Colonel Brandis said. "The president has already authorized the military and the Coast Guard to close the preserve borders."

"You can't—" the commissioner started.

"He has," Captain Sysigns said.

Kir pointed at the other robots in the room. "You'll take no action until this has been confirmed by Congress."

"Kir," Grace Pattermann said, losing patience with her subordinate. "You head the Criminal Division at the HHS. You're not a member of the administration."

"Do you represent the president in this room or the HHS?"

Colonel Brandis said, "I still haven't heard the human tell us anything important."

"You don't think an antivirus is important?" Kir said.

"An alleged antivirus with no apparent proof?"

Chief Laughton felt like he was going to collapse. The commissioner was bright red.

Kir played a recording of an air horn at top volume, and the room fell silent. "Chief Laughton and I are close to finding these people and the antivirus, but we can't do that with a bunch of robots causing hysteria in the humans, and that means no robots on the preserve, and no robot forces amassing on the borders of the preserve."

"You can't expect us to let these orgos—"

Kir interrupted Colonel Brandis, "Humans. You want the commissioner and chief here to call you a bunch of metals?"

"These humans should have been rounded up decades ago," Lieutenant Cray said beside Colonel Brandis. "It's time to just end this whole charade."

Laughton felt like it was all getting away from him—the comfort of easy authority, the calm of living without a daily threat—these things were being crushed. "Twenty-four hours!" he yelled.

Everyone looked at him.

"Twenty-four hours and I'll have the antivirus. All of you, your departments, whatever, give me twenty-four hours."

"With what intelligence—" Agent Spectra started.

"Twenty-four hours," Kir said. "Then we can take this up in Washington."

"You'll just scare everyone into a panic," Laughton said, "if you start closing the borders and moving ships in the harbor."

The room fell silent. It was hard to believe that the robots weren't messaging each other, and they most likely were within their own delegations, no one wanting to show their hand to anyone else, let alone the orgos in the room.

Captain Sysigns said, "I'm not moving my ships. They're already there. That barricade is only going to get tighter."

Grace Pattermann spoke at last. She must have been doing extreme calculations. Since snapping at Kir, she had seemingly withdrawn from the conversation. "Twenty-four hours."

Colonel Brandis threw his hands up. "This is ridiculous. We're under attack, and you want to let them keep at it."

"No," Pattermann said. "I'm saying, an antivirus by tomorrow or the preserve *will* be cordoned off."

"Congress—" Kir said.

"Let's not waste words," Pattermann said. Then looking right at Chief Laughton, she said, "And you don't want to waste any time."

Laughton felt like the whole room was rushing away from him in every direction, his vision growing dark. What the fuck had he gotten himself into?

"Fine," Kir said, and rounded the table. "Come on, Jesse."

He opened the conference room door, and the commissioner followed him out.

Laughton blinked as though waking. The robots were all watching him. Was this what history felt like? A vision of Erica formed in his mind. He didn't know what to do.

He turned and left the room.

Whaat just happened in there?" Laughton said, jogging a few paces to keep up with Kir as he burst out of police headquarters.

"A robot pissing contest," Kir said without slowing his pace.

Laughton jogged again to catch up. "What is that? A power surge?"

Kir stopped short, and turned to his partner. The almost invisible apertures hidden in his eyes widened as some of his anger drifted into laughter. "That's good."

Jesse's own face opened into a grin, the smile spreading through his neck and shoulders. He knew that simply changing the expression on your face could actually change your mood. Why didn't he ever think to do it?

"Did you just make that up?" Kir said.

"Yeah."

"We'll always be inferior copies to you," Kir said.

"Or you need to spend more time with an eight-year-old."

"Yeah," Kir said, nodding. "I do."

Some officers rushed out of the main entrance, breaking the momentary respite. The partners turned as one toward the truck.

"Let's get to the Sisters' warehouse," Laughton said. "Can't imagine McCardy actually went there, but we better make sure." He shook his head as he opened the driver's-side door. "There's no way we're solving this thing in twenty-four hours."

"Like you said," Kir said across the hood, "we just need to find the cure. We'll worry about the killers later."

"Needle in a haystack," Laughton said.

"We need to find the haystack," Kir said.

Laughton thought for a moment, then raised his eyebrows and shrugged. "Well, good thing we're going to see some farmers."

————

The warehouse district could have been a ghost town, although Chief Laughton had been in enough ghost towns to sense there was something here that made it feel inhabited. He realized it was the hum of an HVAC system on the side of one of the nearby buildings, and the orderly row of garbage cans lined up beside a dumpster across the way. In ghost towns, the dumpsters seemed to always be open and overflowing, as though taking out the trash was the last thing everyone did before leaving town.

Kir pointed to a car parked about one hundred yards down the street. Two silhouettes were visible in the front seats. The partners went up to it and knocked on the driver's-side window. Laughton flashed his badge as the window lowered. "Any movement?" he said to the officer in the driver's seat.

The policeman shook his head. "Nothing. We have a quadcopter around the back. No one coming in or out that way either."

"How about a motorbike? See one come by?"

The officer frowned and shook his head. "Naw."

Damn! Laughton thought. He banged on the roof of the car. "Great," he said, "Thanks."

"You want us to come in with you, boss?"

Laughton didn't like the idea of going into a potentially

volatile situation with men he didn't know. "Stay out here," he said. "Anyone comes out, go after them."

"Yes, sir," the officer said.

Laughton and Kir walked away from the vehicle toward the warehouse. "We got people in there?" Laughton said to his partner.

Kir scanned the building for heat signatures. "Five."

Laughton allowed himself to hope that one of them was McCardy despite the absence of a motorbike.

"Ready?" Kir said.

Laughton's phone buzzed. He looked. It was a text from Betty: "Let me know you're all right."

Laughton put the phone away and unsnapped the guard on his gun belt. They started for the entrance, and Laughton's phone buzzed again. This time Betty said, "I'm really scared."

"Betty?" Kir said.

"Yeah."

"You should respond."

"And say—" But the phone buzzed then, and Betty's name popped up on-screen. If he talked to her, he might lose focus. But if things went wrong with the Sisters . . . And that was the problem. Just her calling had his mind in the wrong place. The phone stopped buzzing, and the call was marked as missed. "Come on," he said, ignoring Kir's quiet disapproval.

Laughton knocked on the Sisters' door. He kept his eyes on the ground, unfocused, as he listened, waiting for them to answer.

"They're right inside," Kir said.

Laughton knocked again. No sound came from inside. The HVAC hummed.

"Ready?" Kir said.

Laughton nodded, and put his hand on the grip of his holstered gun. He still hadn't drawn it on the preserve, and he wasn't going to until he had no choice.

Kir punched the door just above the doorknob, denting the metal, the sound echoing on the neighboring buildings. He punched again in the exact same spot, and again, and on the fourth time, the doorjamb broke, releasing the door. He pushed it open, and the loud forceful cough of a double-barreled shotgun burst in Laughton's ears. Kir rocked back. Laughton pulled his gun, adrenaline sharpening his vision. Kir had already absorbed the impact of the shot, and was rushing forward toward the young woman holding the gun who managed to get another shot off, tagging Kir's shoulder as he reached her. He ripped the gun from her hands, and bent the barrel in half like Superman.

The woman looked as though she was going to attack Kir with her bare hands, her face and neck flushed, her arms rigid at her sides.

"Please put your gun away," a female voice said behind Laughton.

Kir turned at the sound.

"You'd never reach me before I fired," the woman said.

Chief Laughton raised his hands, but didn't let go of his pistol. "We're not here to arrest anyone," he said.

"Unless one of you murdered Carl Smythe," Kir said.

Laughton saw a third woman standing back at the desk in the rear. Two men were by one of two vans, its rear doors open, the inside stacked with boxes. "I'm going to put my gun away," Laughton said. He began to move his hand slowly. He half expected the unseen woman behind him to say "Drop it," but she fortunately didn't make a demand the chief would not have met. He snapped his gun back in place, and turned, surprised to find the woman holding him in her sights looked almost identical to the woman at the back of the warehouse near the desk, short, with wide-set narrow eyes. Sisters. Maybe twins. "You don't need that anymore," Laughton said, nodding at the gun.

The woman continued to hold it on him. "What do you want?"

Laughton looked around, trying to keep tabs on everyone. The woman at the back of the warehouse started toward them. The men loading the van seemed happy to let the women handle the police officers.

The woman who had shot Kir with the shotgun was younger than the other two with ice-blue eyes. "Get moving," she yelled at the men by the van.

The men jumped, and then began moving boxes into the van.

Laughton noticed the shelving units toward the back were mostly empty. "Packing?" he said.

"We didn't murder anybody," Twin One said, still holding the gun.

Kir was inspecting the damage where the bullet had torn through his clothes and simul-skin revealing some wires within. "Not for lack of trying," he said.

"Fuck you, metal," the woman who had shot him said.

"You okay?" Laughton said.

"Fine."

"We *are* packing, to answer your question," Twin Two said.

Blue Eyes's mouth dropped open and her eyebrows went up as she glared in surprise at Twin Two, her expression clearly saying "Seriously? You're going to talk to them?" When she got no reaction from the other two women, she stormed off to help loading the van.

Twin One lowered her weapon. "We see what's happening. Plan was to get out before they came for us. So when you show up with a robot punching in our door . . ."

Kir had stripped the ends of a few of the exposed wires and was twisting them together. "I'm one of the good guys," he said. "Can I actually say that out loud?"

"We're not here to arrest you," Laughton said again. "I'm Chief Laughton from Liberty. This is Agent Kir from Health and Human Services. Can we call you something other than the Sisters?"

Twin One shook her head. "No."

"The one who welcomed us with the shotgun is Lysee Martins," Kir said. "These two are Marcy and Jenny Leonard."

"Fucking face recognition," Marcy said.

"So you're not all sisters?" Laughton said.

Marcy said, "How can you bring this shit in here?" She nodded at Kir.

Instead of answering the question, Laughton said, "We've pretty much got twenty-four hours to prevent martial law, and then they really will come for you. We just need whatever you know."

"About what?" Jenny Leonard said. "We didn't have anything to do with Smythe getting killed."

"Honestly," Laughton said, "I'm not even worried about that right now. I need the antivirus for this thing that's killing robots."

"Killer Apps," Jenny said. "They had to be clever."

"Sounds like a human," Kir said, expressing a rare anti-orgo moment. Laughton blinked in surprise. "Puns," Kir said, and Laughton nodded his understanding. It hadn't been anti-orgo, just observational.

"Don't talk to him with that metal here," Lysee yelled from the back of the warehouse.

"She's going to get one of you killed," Laughton said.

"Or save our lives," Jenny said.

"We don't have the antivirus," Marcy said.

"McCardy does, and we know that he was looking to make contact with you. Has he?"

"No," Marcy said with annoyed amusement that said it would be a bad idea if he did. Guess he'd been right to seek out Gary's help.

"Sounds like it would be a bad idea if he did."

The Sisters didn't respond to that.

"You know, we did you a big favor last night," Kir said. He was no longer fiddling with his insides.

"Fuck you, metal," Lysee yelled.

"Lysee!" Jenny chastened.

"You're the one who shot *me*!" Kir called at the angry young woman.

"Okay!" Laughton yelled, and everyone looked at him. "We all want the same thing right now, and that's to keep the robots off the preserve, yeah?" He waited, looking around from person to person. The loaders had stopped again to watch. "They're trying to use this to kill the preserve, so we need that antivirus now."

"We heard about that club," Jenny said. "We didn't know about it before." She looked at Marcy, who blinked her eyes in consent. "We knew Titanium was moving product off the preserve by boat. He's working off some island out past Johns Island. We figured there was enough to go around, but then Carter's deliveries became erratic. We thought he was diverting his supply through Titanium."

"We weren't going to allow that much longer," Marcy said.

"Then why kill Smythe?" Laughton said, hoping to catch them out.

Jenny smiled. "Nice try, Chief. We didn't do that, but Jones thought we did, and ran to Titanium. We figured McCardy must have followed."

Laughton tried to make that fit. If Jones and McCardy thought the Sisters had discovered their disloyalty and were going to kill them, why was McCardy heading for them? He had either approached Titanium unsuccessfully or hoped to convince the Sisters that he wasn't party to Jones's betrayal.

"You have any clearer idea about where Titanium is?" Laughton said.

Jenny's and Marcy's eyes met, but Laughton couldn't tell what had passed between them. "No," Jenny said, her face open and honest.

Laughton looked at Kir. "What do you think?"

Kir looked back at Lysee, who was sitting at the desk, leaning back in the chair, arms crossed across her chest. "Fuck you, metal!" she yelled. "You're lucky they weren't electric tips."

"*She* shot *me*," he said to Jenny and Marcy.

"You did punch down our door."

"We knocked first. You could have opened it."

"Where are you going? Out to your farm?" Laughton said.

Jenny shook her head. "We're going to change scenes for a few days, off the preserve."

Laughton shook his head. "That's not going to work."

"Fix this situation, and we'll come right back," Marcy said.

"Right," Kir said.

"We've got you, don't we?" Jenny said.

Laughton snorted. "Yeah. And all you can give me is that Titanium was taking things out by boat. We already knew that."

Jenny shrugged. "We can only tell you what we know, and that's all we know."

Laughton said nothing, watching her face, but the muscles remained relaxed, no micro-expressions to give away a lie. Titanium had managed to keep the Sisters in the dark.

"You still can't take off," Laughton said. "Don't make me arrest all of you just to keep you where we can find you."

Marcy and Jenny exchanged a look, all of the muscles in their faces tightening in the exact same way, almost like a living mirror. "Aren't your boys in the car out there going to keep tabs on us?" Marcy said. "That's not good enough?"

Laughton wasn't surprised that they had spotted the men outside, but he was disappointed nonetheless.

"And your machine here," Lysee said, rejoining them. "You've got our vans on GPS now, don't you."

"Assuming you didn't burn them out," he said.

"Chief Laughton," Jenny said. "South Carolina is our home and it always has been. You do what you need to do, and we'll be back. But right now we need to do what we need to do."

"I'm going to believe that what you need to do is go to your farm, and if we need you and you're not there, you might not have a farm to come back to."

"Listen, asshole—" Lysee started.

But Marcy stopped her with a raised hand. "Do your job, Chief, and it won't come to that, because if it did, it wouldn't be good for you."

They all let the counterthreat hang in the air. After a moment, Laughton held up his phone. "I need to be able to contact one of you."

Jenny pulled her phone out of her back pocket, and they tapped them together. "Good enough?" Jenny said.

Laughton didn't feel at all that it was good enough, certain if the Sisters didn't want to be found again that he would never

find them. But if things played out in their favor, and the preserve went on, it would be better to have the Sisters as a source
than as enemies. "Sure," he said.

Kir looked at Lysee. "Next time they better be electric tips,"
he said to her.

"Fuck you, metal."

"Ladies," Kir said with a nod of the head and a casual
two-finger salute. He headed out the door.

Laughton watched the whole operation for another minute, yearning for the right question to ask, feeling like there
must be something to glean here, but in the end, he turned
and followed Kir through the broken door frame and into the
daylight.

Outside, the chief crashed from the adrenaline comedown
as it fully registered that shots had been fired. He brought his
hands to his head, and then rubbed them on his thighs, taking
a deep breath and exhaling.

Kir patted him on the back. "I'm the one who got shot,"
he said.

You don't have pain receptors, Laughton thought, but was too
shaken to voice. He remembered Betty's call, and felt guilty for
ignoring it. If things had gone another way in there . . .

He pulled out his phone. She picked up before it had even
rung on his end. "Where are you? Are you okay?" she said.

"I'm fine," he said. He wasn't fine, but Betty's own panic
was too big for him to tell her what was happening.

"What's wrong? You don't sound right," she said, knowing
him too well to be fooled.

"I'm fine," he insisted.

"My phone is exploding. People are saying the army is
invading the preserve. What's happening? I'm freaking out."

"Betty," Laughton said, speaking deliberately. He knew the

best thing was the truth, but he didn't want to panic her more than she already was. "There are governmental delegates here. That's it."

"Why? Where are you? How do you know that's it? They're saying they're closing the roads out of the preserve."

"Betty, I'm telling you. Everything is okay."

There was a pause while Betty tried to gauge if she should believe him, rallying her inner resolve. He knew wherever she was, at the school, at the clinic, that she was the rock, the one who was no doubt reassuring everyone else, but she now needed someone to reassure her. "I'm scared," she said, the panic gone from her voice.

"Listen," he said, "I'm taking care of it."

Her voice grew sharp. "How are *you* taking care of it? What is happening?"

He tried to think how to explain it in the simplest way.

"Jesse?"

"Yes. I'm here. All right." Kir had walked back down to talk to the officers in the unmarked car. "You know we were concerned the government would use the murder to come in to the preserve?"

"Isn't that what's happening?"

"No," he said, shaking his head even though she couldn't see him. "There's a sim going around out there that's killing robots, and they think it came from here, from our dead hacker actually. They're looking for anyone who helped, and an antivirus."

"But they're closing the roads."

"No, they're not," he said, hoping it sounded authoritative. They'd promised him they wouldn't, but he honestly didn't know if it was true.

"Jesse, where are you? Come home."

He sighed. "I'm in Charleston. Kir and I think we might be able to find the antivirus. We've got leads."

"Oh. All right," she said, her voice withdrawing. "Do you want to say hi to Erica?" She lowered her voice. "She's scared too."

Of course she is, Laughton thought, *if you're in a panic*. "Put her on," he said.

"Hi, Daddy," Erica said. She always sounded nervous and far away on the phone. She never wanted to put it up to her ear, worried that she would accidently hit something on the touch screen with her cheek, so speakerphone it was.

"Hey," he said.

"We're at the clinic. There are a ton of people here."

Laughton tried to picture that, but his mind stayed fuzzy. "You okay? You know why people are excited?"

"The robots are coming?" she said.

"No," he said, his heart breaking at the resigned way she said it. "No. I'm taking care of everything. The robots are not coming. This is the preserve."

"Okay. Here's Mommy."

"Erica, wait, you know I love you, right?" But it was Betty again. Erica, rushing off the phone as soon as possible, as usual, hadn't heard him. "Is she okay?" he said to Betty.

"She's nervous, but okay." Her voice grew louder as she took it off of speaker. "Jesse, are you coming home tonight? Are you safe?"

He looked at Kir, the tattered hole in his side. "I might not be home tonight," he said, ignoring the second question. "I'll call you when I can. Just stay calm."

"Okay," she said, and now she sounded a million miles away.

He felt the sorrow in a ball on top of his stomach, the sickness of being an organic man in a robotic world.

"I love you," she said.

"Yeah," he said.

"Be safe." She ended the call.

Laughton went down to join Kir by the unmarked car.

"Okay?" Kir said as Laughton approached.

"Yeah," Laughton said, but it didn't sound very convincing to his ears.

"Charlie and Graham are going to follow the Sisters when they finally take off," Kir said.

"They know you're out here," Laughton said to the men in the car, "so don't go out of your way to not get spotted."

"He told us," the officer in the driver's seat said.

"And call me, if you have anything to report," Laughton said. "Don't talk to anyone else." He held out his phone and they exchanged info.

"Right," the driver said. Laughton didn't know if he was Charlie or Graham.

"Docks?" Kir said to him. Laughton was still distracted by his conversation with his family, and it must have been apparent, because Kir said, "If they were taking it out by boat . . ."

Laughton nodded, and they started walking toward the truck. The chief couldn't help but feel that he had failed in his duties as a husband and father, that he hadn't been there for them. "Erica asked me the other day why they made the preserve."

"What did you tell her?"

"I told her it was easier to feed everybody if they were close together. That it was easier to repopulate, better for her to have human friends, just, I don't know, the things that everyone talks about."

"Don't forget, so that we can get you all in one place and wipe you out once and for all," Kir said.

"I left that one out," Laughton said.

"Look, I can't believe anyone thinks it, but there are a lot of robots that are angry that you were given so much land, and right on the East Coast," Kir said.

"We were here first," Laughton said, cringing for echoing the right-wingers.

"You were," Kir said.

"It kills me to say it," Laughton said, "but we made you."

"You did."

"It's only right we have a place of our own."

"I don't disagree," Kir said. "But . . ."

"What?"

"Most robots don't realize it, but it's still a human world. We may be the majority now, but America—still here. President, Congress, the whole thing. We're robots, and we're still running your government. Your government in which we were considered things, not individuals. We're still speaking English, out loud. We're like colonials after the empire recedes, still living under the empire's rules."

"Sure, by humans for robots."

"Isn't that better than a whole new world?"

"You realize here that *we're* the indigenous people?" Laughton said.

"Right. You're both. The occupying colonial government and the indigenous peoples."

"Yeah. We have it all."

There was a moment of silence, while each partner thought.

"Jesse, you know I'm on your side. That's why I'm here."

"I'm not sure there are sides."

"Protect and serve," Kir said.

"Protect and serve."

"So are we going to the docks?"

"You really think an island?" Laughton said, the corner of one side of his mouth raised in skepticism.

"Got anything else?"

Laughton turned on the truck. "Damn."

Laughton had to call the Charleston dispatcher to find out where the Marine Police Division was located; the GPS couldn't find it. They occupied a small wharf on the Wando River next to a private yachting club. The rusted cranes of the Port of Charleston, like mammoth, long-necked animals preparing to drink, stood to the north. Away to the south, the diamond-shaped towers of the Ravenel Bridge cut peaks in the sky, as they had since they replaced the twentieth-century structures more than one hundred years before. A chain-link fence topped with barbed wire enclosed the police station property, but the gates were open, allowing access to the cracked parking area. Three fifty-foot police boats with sharp bows that were a cross between a shark's snout and a tank sat on tractor trailers outside of a large boathouse.

Laughton and Kir headed for what looked like a bait shop, a small building built out onto the pier. There were two yellow, hard-shelled inflatable boats in the water bearing the word "Police" in large plain type, and another fifty-footer like the ones in the parking lot. The door to the station had a window in the top half, but a closed set of venetian blinds hid any view of the inside. The blinds swung to as Laughton opened the door, slapping back again with a clatter.

There were three metal desks crammed into the small office. They were all coated with the mess of electronics that could be found on every policeman's desk—monitors, keyboards, desktops, laptops, tablets, e-readers—and the ensuing cables that dripped over the backs of the desks to power strips on the floor. One of the desks sported several model boats of a variety of sizes. An oversize photo, too large for the space, hung off-kilter on the wall, showing six men in front of one of the police boats with false grim expressions meant to make them seem imposing.

One of the men from the picture sat at the farthest desk, leaning back in a spring-backed desk chair, salt-and-pepper hair and a gray mustache, his skin the cracked leather of years spent on boats under the sun. Another man, not in the picture, sat in a metal straight-backed chair on the other side of the desk, black, with white hair and beard that formed a kind of mane around his face. "Gentlemen," the man in the desk chair said. Then it registered that one of them was a robot, and both men's expressions tightened for a fraction of a second, almost imperceptible to an untrained eye.

Laughton showed his credentials, and the policeman introduced himself as Chief Barston. The other man wasn't police, but a maintenance worker at the yacht club, James. He seemed at home in the little police station.

"We want to ask you about sims trafficking on the water out here," Laughton said.

James snorted. "Good luck," he said.

"We get a lot of it," Chief Barston said.

"That's *all* we've got out here," James said.

"You and I go fishing, and we're not the only ones," Barston said.

"Yeah, everyone's fishing with a tackle box full of memory sticks."

Barston's eyes flitted to Kir before returning to Laughton. "We get some," he amended.

Laughton pointed to his partner. "You don't have to worry about him."

"I'm not here to police you or anybody," Kir said.

"We do our best," Barston said, shifting in his chair.

"How many boats do you have out?" Laughton said.

Barston smirked. "None. Metals—no offense—Coast Guard shut down the harbor. Not supposed to have any boats out. I sent the boys home."

Laughton exchanged a look with Kir.

"News said they shut the roads down too," Barston said.

"I said no way they going to let us alone out here, just parcel off some land and give it to us," James said. "People should read their history. Metals were made by people as much as they want to forget it, and you can see what people did when they started separating groups out."

Kir said, "My channels are saying that they're preparing for shutdown, but are holding for tomorrow, as we agreed."

"Well, the Coast Guard sure as hell isn't waiting," Barston said. "But they can try all they want to blockade, I'll tell you, someone wants to get through, they can."

"Have you heard of people operating off any of the islands out here?" Laughton said. "An informant told us that there's a new operation on some island."

"A reason that pirates liked these waters," Barston said. "I'm sure there are people on the islands out there."

"Dewees Island," James said.

"Dewees not part of the preserve," Barston said.

"No one knows what's part of the preserve out there." James looked Laughton straight in the eye. "I'm telling you, there are people out on Dewees. Got lights on. Just in the past few weeks." He looked back at Barston. "I don't always stay on-preserve. What the hell you got a boat for otherwise?"

"Would you take us out there?" Laughton said.

Barston held his hands up in front of him. "I'm not breaking a blockade. They complain the Maritime Division's ineffective as it is. I'm not giving them an excuse to shut us down."

James said, "Don't even look at me. I'm a civilian."

Laughton pulled out his phone and opened the maps program. He held it out to James. "Can you show us where Dewees is and where you saw the lights?"

James took the phone. Chief Barston leaned over his desk so he could see as well. James pinched and swiped at the screen until he had the correct island on view, then pointed to the coast at the south end of the island. "There," he said, handing the phone back.

Laughton put a pin there, and put the phone back in his pocket.

"Wouldn't go out there in the daytime," James said. "Coast Guard on patrol."

"They use infrared," Barston said. "Nighttime doesn't matter."

Laughton felt the anxious paranoia of life before the preserve closing around him, something he hadn't realized he felt until he began to live without it. "We'll be careful."

"Got a boat?" James said.

"We don't want to worry you," Laughton said, thinking they'd steal a boat. That way no one else could be held responsible.

"Okay," James said. "Yacht club might have some small boats just tied up over there. Maybe. They might."

Laughton took his phone out again and held it out to Chief Barston. "If you hear anything . . ."

Barston picked up his own phone from the desk, and touched it to Laughton's. "What are you looking for exactly? 'Cause really these waters are a free road for anyone, and we don't get too worried about sims, though don't tell anyone that." He checked Kir for a reaction.

"You hear about the robots dying from that sim?"

"Something," Barston said.

"We think the antivirus might be out on that island. Fix that, and robots don't have an excuse to lock us in."

"They don't need an excuse," James said.

"At least they won't have one," Laughton said.

Barston shook his head. He suddenly looked tired. "Good luck," he said.

"Thank you for your help," Kir said.

James snorted, staring ahead, not looking at them.

"Thanks," Laughton said, and pulled open the door to the outside. The blinds swung again, and rattled as they shut the door behind them. "What do you think?" he said outside.

Kir looked up at the sky. The blue was growing washed-out. "Maybe an hour and a half until sunset."

"And the IR?"

"Risk it?" Kir said. "Chances are good we won't be anywhere near Coast Guard."

"We hope."

"Night is still better," Kir said.

"Then I need to lie down. My face feels like it's peeling off of my head, and my head feels like someone's tightening a metal band around it."

"Where to?"

"I'll sleep in the back of the truck. But let's move it somewhere. Don't want to make things hard for these guys."

"Right," Kir said.

Laughton nodded. They were going to go off the preserve, and through a robot blockade. They'd have no authority and no protection, and while Kir could always call people in, it didn't mean they'd always be friendly. His tired spread over him. What a goddamn mess.

The chief jerked awake and then stayed still, opening his eyes wide, waiting to remember where he was and why he was so damned uncomfortable.

"Jesse."

It was Kir. Laughton sat up, wincing as his back realigned. They had found a parking lot with a charging station not far from the marine police station where they were mostly not visible to the traffic on the street. They'd plugged in the truck, and Kir too, and Jesse had hoped a power nap would clear his head for their river voyage by moonlight. It was dark out now. This part of Charleston wasn't quite as empty as Liberty, but it was empty enough that there was not much by way of artificial light. The charging station was only still active because it was against the law to shut them off. The building it went with was dead.

Kir tapped him on the shoulder. "You ready?"

Laughton took a deep breath and let it out through his nose. Then he rubbed his face with both hands, and shook his head once to clear it. "Yeah," he said, and pulled himself to his feet. He jumped from the back end of the truck and closed the tailgate.

Kir put his hand on Laughton's shoulder, stopping him from going forward. "Jesse, don't take this the wrong way, but when you die, would you want me to stay on until Erica dies?"

"Jesus," Laughton said.

"Really," Kir said. "Because I can. I can live through your grandchildren's lives too. Forever."

"Let's just do this thing. No one's going to die tonight."

"Of course, sure. But seriously, would you want me to be alive to watch over Erica until the end of her life?"

Laughton thought about his father refusing to move to the reserve because of his love for the robot that had been in his life forever. Was the feeling mutual? "I couldn't ask that of you."

"I just—while you slept, thought about what we were talking about, who the world's for, and what's my point if I just go on forever? Why?"

"You've heard Betty talk about school?" Laughton said. "That humans still have great things they can do, and that school can help unlock those things?"

"Yeah."

"Let's be honest," Laughton said. "Who cares? They're never going to grow up and go to work. What do they really need to learn? Why bother teaching them?"

"Why bother making more of them?"

"Exactly."

"So you're pretty much against everything your wife works for."

Laughton grinned. "Don't tell her that."

"Oh, I shouldn't have just sent that text message?" Kir said.

"Metal face," Laughton said.

"Meatbag," Kir said.

"My dad always said the robots were meant to serve us, and then they failed. Yet the most important person in the world to him after my mother is a robot."

"And you and your sister."

"Maybe."

They let that hang for a moment.

Kir said, "Mine said that robots were meant to serve people too, which is why he deactivated when he no longer had a human to serve."

"So everyone's trying to perpetuate this thing," Laughton said. "Our race, our way of living, our history, our legacy . . ."

"Still all about you," Kir said.

"Why?" Laughton said.

Kir shook his head. "I don't know."

"Why should any of us go on?"

"Meaning of life?"

"If we can't live forever, why bother, but if we can live forever, why bother?"

"Why?"

"Maybe we just can't think of doing anything else."

"What does Erica think?"

"I don't know. She's eight."

"What does that mean?"

Laughton wasn't sure. Erica understood things he couldn't comprehend. She was wise and kind, like her mother. "I guess Erica is why. It's for her. To keep it all for her, so that she can make the decision herself, but my job, life, whatever, is to keep it all for her."

Kir said, "Mine too."

Laughton digested that, feeling how true it was. It made him think of his own parents. If Erica was his reason not only for living, but for even just trying to maintain the world as best he could, was that true for his parents too? "My father lost everyone in the plagues," he said, "but then his politics are so important to him that he won't come live with what's left of his family on the preserve."

"Maybe that's his way of trying to save the world for you."

"It's pretty stupid."

"How about ending up in a shoot-out?" Kir said.

"Fuck you," Laughton said, but it made him consider what he was about to go do. If he ended up dead, how would that make the world better for Erica? "None of it will matter if I let this case shut down the preserve." He looked at Kir, really looked at him with all of his acumen for reading faces, and the robot's false features were suffused with concern. Tears stung Laughton's eyes as he said, "I would absolutely want you to be there for Erica for her whole life. It . . . Yeah."

"Yeah," Kir said.

They had decided to walk so the truck didn't give them away at the yacht club. They might have silent local approval from the club, but if someone other than James came by, saw the truck, and called the police, they'd be hard-pressed to present a legal explanation for commandeering a boat.

There were no lights on at the yacht club. It wasn't the kind of place that had a restaurant, especially if its main clientele had been robots pre-preserve. Unlike at the police dock, the gate here was closed, and for a moment Laughton was afraid they'd have to break in, but when he checked, he found that it had been left unlocked. Whether that had been for them or was standard procedure, he didn't know, but he thought the former. Either way, it made their lives easier.

"What are we looking for?" Laughton said. He realized he'd whispered even though there wasn't anyone around.

"Something small with an engine," Kir said.

"I don't know anything about boating."

"When we find the one we want, I'll download instructions."

"They're not like cars. You need to actually steer them," Laughton said.

Kir didn't respond. That didn't matter to a robot. The internet explained all, which meant that robots knew all, were all knowing.

There was a deck along the front of the clubhouse that wrapped around the side of the building, and most likely, to the boats. They clattered up the uneven wooden boards.

Laughton's toe got caught on one, and he almost fell, skipping with the momentum to remain on his feet.

"Careful," Kir said. "You're delicate."

"Fuck you," Laughton said.

It was too dark to see much more than outlines, but when they reached the back of the building, the paler sky made a clear divide across the water, separating the landscape from the heavens. There were six piers extending into the river, each with a pair of boats attached, mostly in the thirty-to-fifty-foot range, small yachts for a day's pleasure cruise, but they too were nothing but outlines for the chief.

"What are they?" Laughton said, knowing his partner was seeing everything with the help of his night vision.

"Too big," Kir said.

They were almost at the end of the dock. The slight sound of splashing water as the boats shifted the few inches their tethers allowed made him think of the time that Betty got him to go night kayaking. Erica ended up in his boat. She had leaned over constantly to look down at the water, which had thrown off the weight of the kayak. By the end, his back hurt so much, he could barely get out of the boat.

"There," Kir said.

At the very end of the dock, three flat-bottomed canoes with outboard motors were tied rather haphazardly to one cleat.

"Do we have to worry about the noise?" Laughton said.

"No. This is perfect. You stay back near the motor, and the heat of the engine should help mask you on IR. Anyone looking will see a boat operated by a robot, and probably leave us alone." Robots showed hot in one or two places depending on the cpu placement, while humans were hot all over.

Laughton didn't think that sounded too likely. He imagined the Coast Guard would be stopping every boat they came across, but he didn't see any way around it.

Kir was unwinding one of the ropes on the cleat. "Jump down and figure out which boat this goes to," he said.

Laughton found a ladder of boards nailed directly to one of the dock's supporting posts. He stepped into one of the boats. It immediately wanted to get away from him, and he had to pull it back toward the dock with his leg while still hanging on to the ladder. Once it was below him again, he stepped down fully into the boat. He squatted, trying to keep his weight low. The boat didn't feel very steady to him, but what did he know? He pulled on the thick rope tied to the front of the boat. "Is this it?" he shouted.

"Pull more," Kir said.

He pulled harder, but the rope felt stuck—it must be the wrong one—then it came loose so fast, he almost fell backward. There was the splash as the other end of rope hit the water, and as he pulled it into the boat, it was wet and heavy.

Kir climbed down the ladder and hopped in.

Laughton piled the rope at his feet. "Ready?"

Kir answered by simply going to the engine and turning it on. The boat vibrated and shook, but it steadied as he backed them slowly away from the dock, bumping into the neighboring boats slightly. They cleared the other boats, and Kir started to turn them around so they were facing away from the dock. The pitch of the motor rose, and they started moving, a light breeze causing the chief to shiver.

As they picked up speed, and the wind grew stronger, the chief had to actively push down the anxiety tightening in his chest from moving fast while blind. *Kir can see*, he reminded himself over and over. *Kir can see. We're not going to hit anything*. The bow of the boat lifted out of the water, and a fine mist hit them every time the boat bounced on the river. The chief's eyes watered against the wind. Instead of looking directly into it, and the blackness before them, he tried to watch the banks. On the mainland, outlines of palm trees were negative black space against the barely illuminated black sky. The squat dark boxes of buildings at times broke up the tree line. Across the way, the trees were denser, willows and oaks and other native species forming a wall.

Laughton put his hand in his pocket to double-check that the two magazines of electric-tipped bullets he had pulled from the truck's lockbox were still there. The cartridges currently in his gun were standard bullets, but he wanted to be prepared if the people at the other end of this trip were metals. Kir had his built-in Tasers if needed.

They went under the Ravenel Bridge, and then there weren't any recognizable landmarks that the chief could see in the dark. "Do you know where we're going?" Laughton called.

"Yes," Kir shouted back.

They pressed on, the boat hopping and jumping across the water. Laughton's anxiety seeped away, and he was left bored. *How much longer?* he thought, and smiled. This was no doubt how Erica felt on every long road trip. Betty had such little patience for the age-old "Are we there yet?"

Eventually Kir slowed the boat, the bow lowering and the ride growing less bumpy. "Are we close?" Laughton said.

"No. But we're entering narrower channels. Can't go out on the ocean side. Coast Guard out there, and this boat isn't really meant for oceangoing. We'll run through these channels up to Dewees."

Banks had closed in on either side of them, increasing the darkness. Alternate waterways opened to the left and to the right. Small grass-covered islands drifted by, some no larger than the building that housed the police in Liberty, good only for birds and whatever snails, crabs, oysters, and fish made their lives at the water's edge. Some larger islands, covered with heavier vegetation, were expansive enough to not seem like islands at all. They went under several bridges. Road signs could be seen to either side, the sharp straight lines of their silhouettes feeling improbable in the surroundings.

"This is a smuggler's paradise out here," Laughton shouted over the sound of the motor. "They could be anywhere."

"Most of these islands have nothing on them, and the solidity of their land is deceptive in the dark. They're more like marshes."

Laughton knew all too well the convenience and advantages of using preexisting buildings. It made sense that if nothing had ever been built on an island, it was unlikely to be in use now.

"Dewees is also at the edge of the preserve," Kir said.

"Safety in the borderlands."

"Let's hope."

Laughton yawned. This better be it. He didn't want to spend the last night of the preserve's existence in a boat more than one hundred miles from Betty and Erica.

Eventually Kir said, "Almost there."

Chief Laughton looked up. There were a few dark masses in front of them, but one appeared much larger than the others. "Where are we going to land?" he said.

"There's an old ferry dock here on the south side of the island," Kir said.

"What if the sims people are using it?"

"We can pull into an inlet that snakes a good way into the center of the island. Might be able to push through the grasses on one of the banks, but not without getting wet."

Laughton thought about going into a situation with wet shoes and socks. The idea was uncomfortable, but was that enough to take the risk on the dock. "I guess scan the dock when we're in sight," he said.

"Wimp," Kir said.

There was moonlight now, so Laughton could see the dock as they approached it, a long letter "L" breaking from the island. A portion of the dock was covered, a pitched roof on posts. A small yacht was docked.

"Anything?" Laughton said.

"Let's try it," Kir said. "I've been shot already today. What are a few more holes?"

"But I haven't been, and those bullets do a lot more damage to me."

Kir adjusted the engine to the lowest setting. It still made noise, but it was more like a lion's purr than a growl. Laughton took a deep breath. He could smell the ocean here, its salty brine. Talk about being out of his jurisdiction.

Kir pulled the boat around the yacht to the side of the dock that was facing the island. Three other small motorboats were tied up there. "Get up there with that rope," Kir said.

"Watch your tone," Laughton said. The familiar joking helped cut some of the tension. Once he was up on the dock on solid ground, he felt everything grow sharp. His headache receded into a heavy throb. He tied off the boat in what he hoped approximated some kind of boatman's knot.

Kir joined him on the dock.

"How big is this island?" Laughton said. "We doing this on foot?"

"Only so much of the island was ever built on."

"If you say so," Laughton said. "But if it comes to it, you're carrying me."

"Not on your life," Kir said. They clopped along the dock. Then Kir stopped suddenly, grabbing Laughton's sleeve, pulling him round.

"What?"

"Got your flash?" Kir said.

Laughton took it from his belt. "Yeah."

"Shine it over there. And start your camera."

Laughton pushed the button on his body camera and then turned the flashlight on, painting the boats with its beam until he saw what had stopped Kir. There was somebody lying in one of the boats.

Kir jumped down into the boat while Laughton remained up top, his free hand on his holstered weapon. But if Kir's jump hadn't woken the man, he didn't think he'd need it.

Kir adjusted the man's head so it could be seen. It was Sam McCardy. A black hole sat at the bridge of his nose between his eyes.

"Guess he chose Titanium after all," Laughton said. "Wrong choice."

"Guess we're in the right place," Kir said.

"How recent?"

Kir let the body lay back and then lifted one of its arms, measuring the resistance. "Twelve hours maybe." He started going through McCardy's pockets, tossing the contents onto the body as he found them—a phone, a key fob, a second phone. He patted down the rest of the body, then pulled off the shoes and checked the heels, and pulled out the innersole. No memory stick.

He picked up the phones, and climbed out of the boat. He handed one to the chief while hitting the home button on the one in his hand. The screen lit up, throwing light on his expressionless face, the simul-skin appearing unnaturally flat.

Laughton turned off his flashlight. He tried the phone, but it wouldn't turn on. "Mine's dead," he said.

Kir scanned the screen of the phone in his hand. "Last four phone calls were numbers, no contact info. Eleven last night, two just after 2:00 a.m. and one at 6:04."

"Must have been his last call. Try them?"

Kir swiped through the screens. "No email on this. Internet memory empty . . ."

"So it was really just a phone."

"Let me hold the other one," Kir said, handing the first phone to Laughton. He opened a port on the inside of his wrist, pulled out a short wire, and plugged it into the bottom of the dead phone. It took half a minute for the display to come on.

"Should I try these numbers?" Laughton said. "We might get a hit."

"Or alert the killer that we're on the island."

"We should at least call it in," Laughton said, reaching for his own phone. "Get some backup on the way."

"Wait," Kir said, scrolling through McCardy's second phone. "Looks like he was good at keeping his email clean. Or he had a web-based account. There's not much more than junk mail. It's the opposite of what most people's email looks like. Good way to keep it messy."

"I'm going to call this in," Laughton said.

Kir shook his head. "Let's see what we've got first. All those departments in that meeting today, ready to sweep in . . ."

"You think this is the government?"

"Let's just wait to call it in."

"Smythe was into radical human terrorism. We might be on our way to a psycho splinter group."

"I'm not sure that would be better."

"Well, I'm not going in with nobody knowing," Laughton said. He tapped his phone.

"Betty?" Kir said.

"Mathews. My deputy." His attention shifted to the phone. "Mathews."

"Chief," Mathews said.

"Mathews, listen. Kir and I are on Dewees Island."

"Is that part of the preserve?"

"Don't worry about that," Laughton said. "If you don't hear from me in . . ." How big was this island? How long would it take to get a read on the place? "If you don't hear from me by midnight, call the commissioner and tell him where we are. Only the commissioner. Talk directly to him."

"Got it. You okay?"

"I've got Kir with me," Laughton said, which wasn't really the answer to the question.

"Be safe," Mathews said.

Laughton hung up. "Where to?"

Kir took both phones and tucked them into a pocket.

"Just need to follow the road," Kir said.

The dock met the island at what must have once been a gravel parking lot, now covered in a scattering of shrubs and grasses. Once on the road, the surrounding trees cut Laughton's visibility down to almost zero. "I can't see a fucking thing," he said.

"Just keep walking straight, and I'll direct you."

"Well, is there any chance anyone's around?"

Kir remained silent for a moment, and then said, "We're good for now."

Laughton turned his flashlight back on, and swung it around to get a sense of their surroundings. The trees were spaced out, the ground around them littered with branches and downed trees. What was almost a barricade built from this detritus lined the roadway. Someone was keeping the path clear. "Must get a lot of hurricanes," Laughton said. There was a flash as the beam of his flashlight caught something reflective. Following it back, he saw an owl on a branch, a large flat face outlined in black, making its eyes seem even larger than they were. It was indifferent to their presence.

He flicked the flash off, and for a moment, he was even blinder than before. He reached in front of him instinctively, even though he had seen only a moment before that there was nothing in his path. When his eyes adjusted, he realized he could see better than he had thought originally, enough to at least see the direction of the road.

They went on in silence. The island was strangely silent as well, no sound of animals or insects. In fact, Laughton realized that he wasn't being plagued by insects at all, no mosquitos or gnats. At least there was that. His mind turned to alligators then. They stayed near the water, he reassured himself, not knowing if this was true.

The degree of darkness to their left lightened, and soon Laughton could see the outline of the trees against the night sky. "What's over there?" he said.

"Waterway that cuts through almost half of the island. Marsh all around it. We couldn't really go that way if we wanted to."

"It's quiet out here," Laughton said.

"Strange, isn't it?"

"Get used to life on the preserve."

"We're not on the preserve," Kir said.

They continued down the road. It was hard to gauge how long they'd been walking. In the dark, it felt like miles, but it probably hadn't even been one mile.

"There," Kir said.

Laughton squinted as though that would help in the night. "What?"

"A light."

Laughton saw it a minute later. It was more than just a light. It must have been a whole building of lights. "What is it?" he said.

"Used to be a resort."

The sight line opened up to their right, and Laughton realized they were only a few hundred feet from the open water. The resort building looked like two enormous houses joined by an enclosed bridge. One of the buildings was dark, but the ground floor of the other showed lights in all of the windows.

They stopped at a cluster of palm trees. "Any hot spots?" Laughton said.

"Can't tell," Kir said.

To the right of the building, a large fenced-in area that had once been tennis courts was currently being used as a helicopter landing pad. Laughton pointed. "We better neutralize that before going in."

Kir agreed by heading in that direction. Laughton jogged a few steps to catch up. He felt exposed in the open, but it didn't seem like there were any lookouts. Why would there be? The island was about as isolated as you could get. Titanium wouldn't be expecting visitors.

They circled the tennis courts to the entrance, and crossed to the helicopter. Black tape had been stretched along the helicopter's side to obscure printed lettering. Chief Laughton picked at the corner of the tape, managing to peel it up with his fingernail. He pulled it off with one long tug to reveal the words "Coast Guard."

"Coast Guard?" he said.

Kir shook his head and shrugged. "Maybe they're following the same lead we are."

"Right," the chief said with an ironic half smile. "And hiding their identity?"

"But the Coast Guard? Brandis I would have expected."

Laughton closed his eyes to think. If the Coast Guard was here *with* Titanium . . .

He remembered the Sisters said Titanium was moving product through the harbor. The Sisters had the trucking routes under their control, but not the water. If there were patrol boats out . . ."That's why Sysigns was the first at the club," he said. "The Coast Guard is giving Titanium's shipments protection on the water, probably for a nice percentage."

"Or Sysigns is Titanium."

"Or that."

Kir was silent for a moment as he calculated. "No wonder Sysigns was ready with his blockade."

"I don't know what that has to do with Smythe's murder," Laughton said. "And McCardy's, I guess."

Kir pulled open the pilot's-side door, and hopped up. There was the sound of metal crunching, and when he hopped back down, he dropped a piece of the control panel on the ground. "No one's taking that anywhere," he said.

"And if they *are* here officially?"

"HHS will pay for it."

Laughton smirked. Sure they would. "Plan?"

"Lay of the land?"

Laughton pulled out his gun, released the magazine, and switched it out for the electric tips. They'd hurt humans just as much as regular bullets, but if Sysigns was here, he'd need the electric ones too. He left his holster unsnapped. "Let's do it," he said.

They approached the building with caution, bent at the knees and hunched over. The first floor of the building was actually one flight up, the whole resort built on stilts, as was necessary on an island that no doubt flooded often. A wide porch ran along the front of the building and along one of the sides. The sound of waves crashing in the distance made Laughton feel very far away from home. When was the last time he'd seen the ocean?

There was no easy way up other than the front stairs. They placed each foot carefully, guarding against the steps' groans and creaks. Without speaking, they split on the porch, going in opposite directions. Laughton stayed close to the wall, pausing just before each window, then peeking, seeing where he could, some with lights on, some with curtains closed. The rooms were suites, a combined kitchen and living room with bedrooms to either side. He reached the end of the building without having seen anybody. The far half of the complex, across the dark pit of an empty pool, was completely black. Looking out from that height, the wide expanse of the ocean was on view, the moon casting enough light to show the moving water, the stars like an inverted, patterned bowl above.

Laughton hurried back, not worried about being seen now that he knew the rooms were all empty. Kir wasn't in sight. He must have rounded the corner to surveil the side porch. Laughton knew he should wait for him, but the complete lack of security so far suggested that Titanium or the Coast Guard or whoever was on the island wasn't concerned about intruders. He decided to try his luck at the double-door entrance. The doors were unlocked. He opened one just enough to see the room within. It was like a cross between a hotel lobby and a great room at a lodge. It was also empty. He let the door close, and was startled to find Kir right beside him.

"Two suites that way are occupied," Kir said. "At least three figures in each, all robots except for one human as near as I can tell."

"Guess we should knock and say hi," Laughton said.

"It's only polite, since we've come all this way."

Laughton pulled out his gun. "Okay," he said.

It was quiet inside. The sound of the ocean was no longer audible. Without speaking, they again split up; Laughton went to the right, and Kir headed for the back of the room. It felt good to be working together, the easy, natural way they seemed to be one mind, knowing each other's rhythms, knowing their roles. So many times they had gone into complicated situations together.

The hall to the right was clear, which was to be expected. Kir emerged from a door behind what must have been the front desk. He nodded once. It was clear.

They converged on the left-hand hallway, which led to the suites where Kir had seen the suspects. Laughton tried doorknobs on the inside set of doors, but all were locked, and none opened at the attempted intrusion. They reached the third door, and Kir stopped. "This is it."

They looked at each other. Laughton shrugged. Kir knocked. There was a pause.

Then the door opened. It was a robot with a familiar face.

"You," Laughton said. He realized now why those robots who had sat down with Jones at K-B's club were familiar. They were the same robots who had staked out Sam and Smythe's house. This robot.

"What—" the off-the-shelf face started, and then pulled back when he saw it wasn't who he expected, freezing, unable to compute what he should do.

Kir used the opportunity to push into the suite, Laughton right behind.

"What is— Kir," the robot standing in the center of the

room said when he saw them. As they suspected, it was Captain Sysigns, the short robot from the Coast Guard. "I didn't know you were cleared for this base."

Kir grinned at the attempt to act as though this was an official stronghold.

Laughton ignored the robot, however, captivated by the figure sitting on the couch, a young woman with a bulky exosuit, the last person he would have expected anywhere near this: Cindy Smythe.

"You're in California," Laughton said to her.

"I assure you, Chief, I'm not."

Laughton remembered Mathews's comment that it was so hard to find her, she must be a hacker too, and it clicked. "Titanium," he said.

"I'm impressed," she said. "I didn't think anyone would find us out here."

"No one has," Sysigns said.

There was a knock on the door, and the off-the-shelf robot answered it, admitting three more robots in Coast Guard uniforms, each the same seven-foot model used by the army. There was a whiz and a buzz, and Kir collapsed, his heavy form hitting the floor with a sharp thud. Laughton flinched. The situation had just gotten very bad.

Captain Sysigns lowered his arm as the Taser wire that had emerged from his finger began to retract. "Chief Laughton," Sysigns said. "You might want to put your gun away."

"I'd like to hold on to it," Laughton said.

Two of the guard robots started to edge into the room. Laughton stepped back so he was almost against the wall, no way for them to get behind him.

"Captain," Cindy Smythe said, her brows knit in anger. "What the fuck?"

"Couldn't risk any messages out," Sysigns said, keeping his eyes on Chief Laughton.

"I have this whole place shielded," Cindy Smythe said.

"Any agreement we come to with Chief Laughton will still be valid when Kir wakes up," Sysigns said.

Laughton made an effort to ignore all the robots in the room, including Sysigns. "You killed your brother?" he said to Cindy Smythe.

Smythe's anger deepened at that, her lips narrowing. "Of course not. Sam killed Carl."

"Yeah, we noticed Sam in a boat on the way in."

"Sam ended his life the second he killed Carl."

And why would Sam kill his closest friend and business partner? Laughton thought. The virus. "Your brother's the source of the virus, and Sam tried to stop him releasing it."

"Carl was always too radical. If he'd told me about the virus, I would have tried to stop him too. Probably why he didn't tell me. Of course, Sam's high morals disappeared as soon as he realized we could sell the antivirus to the entire using community."

"He tried the Sisters, and then you."

"Like anyone would sell the antivirus. It would kill our business if robots felt they couldn't trust our sims, and we were then going to hold them ransom. No, this needs to go out free."

"Enough," Sysigns said, and stepped toward the chief, who raised his gun.

"Slowly," Cindy Smythe said.

"People know I'm here," Laughton said.

"And it turned out Titanium got you," Sysigns said. "But who's Titanium?"

Laughton's chest was so tight, it was strangling him. He took shallow breaths through his nose.

"This can still work out for everyone," Cindy Smythe said.

"He already shut down a third of our operation," Sysigns said.

"I'm not here about the sims," Laughton said.

"Tell that to Kawnac-B," Sysigns said.

Cindy Smythe stood. The motion was jerky, like low-order robots from earlier generations, the pistons and motors lifting her body, forcing the joints to bend. "You can have Sam," she said. "Your case is closed—"

There was a movement at the corner of Laughton's vision, and he turned, and shot one of the oversize robots as it reached for him. Sysigns must have sent the order to end this his way. The robot went down, blocking the advance of the two behind him, which allowed Laughton to drop each of them. His elbow hurt from the recoil, having shot one-handed. His lungs burned and he felt light-headed. It was pure instinct that caused him to jump back, tripping on Kir's body, as Sysigns's Taser uncoiled, the end hitting the wall where Laughton had been standing.

"Sysigns!" Cindy Smythe barked, holding the robot back, the exo-suit giving her enough strength to hold him. "Get out of here. I have this."

"You don't think shutting us down will be a huge political bargaining chip?" the robot said. "Get Brandis off their backs?"

"The cure will be enough."

Laughton struggled to untangle himself from his partner. He brought up his gun, trying to shoot at the same time, but he ended up just shooting the floor.

"You wait," she spat at Laughton, and to Sysigns, "Get out of here." She had a gun in her hand now.

The captain looked at the bodies on the floor, and decided

it was better to clear out. He started toward the door, but the robot bodies made it difficult to move.

Laughton was able to get to his feet, but Cindy Smythe had him covered.

"Don't, Chief," she said.

Sysigns had the door open wide enough for him to leave.

Laughton watched him go, feeling like he had bungled this whole operation, but at the same time, no longer knowing what the operation was about. He turned to face Titanium, who lowered her weapon.

"You've got the antivirus," Laughton said.

"Yes."

"So I just let you and Sysigns go?"

"Will *he* agree to that?" Titanium said, nodding at the still-disabled robot on the floor.

"I don't know that I agree to that."

"Which part?"

At that moment, the Coast Guard robots started to come alive.

"You better go," Cindy Smythe said. "No way to change their orders."

Laughton looked at Kir. How could he leave him? And Titanium. She'd be gone. The first robot was pushing himself up. "Give the cure to Kir when he wakes up," he said.

"Right," she said, a hint of sarcasm in her voice. The chief couldn't tell if she was laughing at the idea of relinquishing the antivirus or the suggestion that she'd still be there when Kir woke up.

He couldn't wait to work it out. If he wanted any chance at Sysigns, he had to believe the latter. The antivirus would be good, but a corrupt robot official would be even better. He jetted from the room without another word.

The chief figured Sysigns had to have gone for the helicopter first. He wondered what time it was, if Mathews already had people on the way. He pulled out his phone, but it wouldn't come on. The whole building was running interference.

Outside, the ocean sounded loud. He couldn't see Sysigns anywhere, but he couldn't see very far at all. He started down the stairs and then headed in the direction of the helicopter, hoping he wasn't passing by Sysigns hidden nearby.

When he got to the helicopter, he found it empty. Sysigns was moving very fast, and he only had one other way off the island—the landing. Laughton started to run. His ankle complained, a gnawing twinge each time his foot landed. His chest began to hurt, the air at the back of his throat feeling impossibly cold.

He did his best to stay on the road. He recognized that the darkness in front of him wasn't quite as black as the darkness to either side, and that helped.

By the time the landing was in sight, Laughton expected to hear a motor start, but he was amazed to find that Sysigns was only just heading down the pier toward the boats. Laughton stopped, and shot, not with any hope that he would hit his target, but that the surprise would stop the robot long enough for Laughton to get to him.

It worked. The robot turned and saw him.

And Laughton felt very exposed. At least the moon, reflecting off the water, evened the odds a little, allowing the chief to see, but it wasn't with the clarity the robot could manage with his night vision and infrared. Laughton squatted next to the nearest post, using it for limited cover. He'd taken four shots in the suite and another warning shot just now. That left him ten rounds in the magazine plus the spare in his pocket, and the regular bullets as well. If he hadn't taken the Coast Guard captain down before he'd emptied his first magazine, he probably would be dead anyway.

Laughton crept around the post he was hiding behind, so that he was hanging off the edge of the dock, his toes burning as they stretched to maintain a hold on the three-inch lip of the pier on the water side of the post. The sound of Sysigns's approach was restrained, a step, a pause, a step. After all, Laughton's appearance on the pier could only mean he escaped unlikely odds back in the suite, and that meant that the chief was dangerous. Captain Sysigns was duly cautious.

Laughton's fingers and toes were now burning so badly that he didn't think he could maintain his position any longer. And he definitely couldn't take a shot. He was worried he'd lose hold of his gun, and if that happened, he had no hope of surviving this. He looked down to see that there was a small boat about five feet beneath him. He lowered his gun hand to the boards and let one leg hang down. Then he ran his hand down the pole, praying against splinters, and lowered his other leg so that he was hanging from the edge of the dock, and could step into the boat without a clunk.

The robot's steps on the dock were almost even with the chief's boat.

All Laughton needed to do was land one shot. One good shot, and the electric shock should shut Sysigns down like it had the robots inside. He took aim, waiting for Sysigns's silhouette to appear above him. He had this, he told himself. He had this. Provide the cure *and* shut down a corrupt Coast Guard . . . the preserve, everyone he knew, was saved.

Sysigns stepped forward and then he was there. Laughton squeezed the trigger, but Sysigns dodged the shot and jumped for the boat. Laughton took another shot, but the target was moving, and he was too rattled to track it. The shot went wild.

Laughton struggled to not fall overboard when Sysigns landed in the boat. The next boat was only about two feet away from the one they were in. Laughton stepped over into it, wobbling and waving his hands to maintain his balance as he put all of his weight forward on the foot in the second boat, and turned, taking aim again.

"You're dead," Sysigns said.

Laughton shot, but the wires of Sysigns's Taser snaked toward him at the same time. He dodged, and the shot missed its mark. Everything was happening very fast, but it seemed like each moment was crawling by, the whole thing happening under water. Even the sounds felt muted.

"How do you think you could hide your involvement in this?" Laughton said.

Sysigns jumped in to the same boat with Laughton. "Involvement in what? Finding the cure?" he said, grabbing at Laughton's gun hand as the chief raised it. He was able to slap it away, but Laughton was able to maintain his grip on the weapon, and pull his hand back so that the robot didn't have a hold on him.

Then Sysigns jumped, which caused the boat to shoot toward the dock, landing Laughton on his back, the edge of the boat catching him in the shoulder blade, tingles shooting down his arm. The robot was on top of him, the damn machine heavy, making it hard to breathe. Laughton tried to hold back Sysigns's hands with his empty one, but his strength was no match for the soldier robot. Sysigns's hand closed around his throat, while his other hand reached for the gun.

Laughton was choking, and not even able to cough. His

eyes rolled up in their sockets, and he strained to aim the gun. He shot once into the side of the boat as Sysigns slammed his hand against the boat bottom. Laughton tried to roll, and the motion threw Sysigns off just enough that the chief was able to raise his arm, rotate his wrist, and take a shot.

This time the bullet grazed Sysigns, the electric charge causing a short, but not a shutdown. Still, the few seconds were enough for Laughton to get out from under him, choking, gasping, coughing, his free hand around his own neck, as though holding it would somehow prevent the pain.

He blinked, his vision turning black for a moment before coming back into focus. The boat wobbled. Sysigns was rising. Laughton turned his head, raised his gun, and shot as the robot leapt at him. This bullet hit him square in the chest, and the charge dropped him like it had dropped his men.

Laughton fell onto his side, coughing. At one point it felt like he was going to cough out his insides, and he was almost wishing to vomit while struggling to get enough air. A sound, out of place, was coming from somewhere nearby, mechanical, no, electric.

He was able to stop coughing, but still had all of his attention focused on breathing. The stars up above were calming, comforting. He pulled himself up into a sitting position, leaning his back against the side of the boat. Sysigns was slumped in an odd pile. As always, Laughton noted how a robot, when shut down, became a thing. When people slept, they were still people, breathing, moving, living. Robots were just things, things that ruled the world.

The sound was coming again, and Laughton realized it was his phone. He was far enough from the building's jamming signal. He put the gun down beside him, and pulled it out. It was Mathews.

"Chief? Chief? Are you okay? You there?"

Laughton tried to say yes, but all he was able to do was cough again.

"Chief!" Mathews was almost in a panic. "They're on their way," he said. "They're on their way."

Laughton took a stuttered, gasping breath, filling his chest. "Good," he said, a croak. "Good."

The cleanup was messy. Mathews had gotten in touch with the commissioner, and the commissioner had known enough to send a human force, so, despite the scene being off the preserve, it was the preserve that got to control the scene. They brought inhibitors, which kept all of the robots shut down. Two young men helped Laughton get Sysigns out of the boat and back to the resort. Titanium was gone. She must have had another way off the island. She *had* left the antivirus in Kir's hand—a white stick to counter the red one that was causing so much damage—and she must have shot the robots again, Laughton realized; otherwise they would have come after him. In any case, it seemed like a deal was a deal, so Laughton thought it was easier to not mention that she had ever been there. The only way this was going to go their way was if it could be all tied up. Once the scene was under control, the commissioner called the army. Laughton figured Brandis would probably love tearing down one of his counterparts almost as much as tearing down humans.

Laughton and Kir snuck back to the boat they had commandeered from the yacht club. They would have to face the colonel and the rest of the robot panel from the day before soon enough—in fact, they received a message not long after leaving the island demanding their presence at police headquarters that afternoon—so they took the opportunity to slip away even if it was only delaying the inevitable. After all, they needed to return the boat and retrieve the truck.

The wind from the speed of the boat made Laughton's eyes water, little rivulets of tears flowing from the outside corners of his eyes back along his temples. It was chilly, but in a way that was refreshing instead of discomforting. The groan of the motor made conversation difficult. Instead, the chief detached his mind, letting the wind and the water and the landscape that had been invisible to him on their night journey wash over his thoughts, suppressing them.

"Look!" Kir yelled, pointing ahead of them, taking the boat down to a whine and then to a grumble.

Laughton tried to follow Kir's sight line, seeing nothing but the oscillating water. Then he saw one, two dorsal fins crest about seventy yards away, describing a gentle arc as they slipped once more beneath the waves. Dolphins. Waiting in anticipation, he kept his eyes on the spot where they had disappeared. Kir cut the engine and joined the chief at the front of the boat. "Breathe," the robot said, but before Laughton could follow his advice, the two fins appeared again, much closer than he had expected them. They were two different sizes and very close together.

"I think one of them's a baby," Laughton said.

The dolphins were just feet away then, and one was definitely a juvenile. They circled, and sped under the boat, appearing on the other side, rising and falling again and again as they explored this novelty.

"Erica will be so jealous," Laughton said.

"Watching you watch them means more to me than they do," Kir said.

That made Laughton miss Erica all the more. That's what he'd have felt if she'd been there. Did that mean Kir saw him as a child? He didn't like that. "I'm not a child," he said.

"I only meant I like to see you happy. Haven't seen that in a while. Betty will be jealous."

The robot meant that he loved him. And Laughton loved Kir too. If he stopped and reflected that Kir was a machine, and that this fact had created the preserve to separate them, he began to wonder if the whole project was a mistake. What was that teaching Erica? That segregation was the only answer to differences? There was ample evidence of hate between robots and humans, which presupposed there could be love, and killing went in all directions.

The dolphins made another pass, and he wondered what the dolphin mother was thinking, showing them to her calf. They dove.

Laughton waited and waited, and when he finally caught sight of them, they were already sixty yards away. He looked at Kir. The robot was watching him.

"You can't plan for this," Laughton said, trying to put his feelings into words. "Even if you go looking for it, you can't plan."

"Like humans," Kir said.

Laughton thought back over the last few days. "Humans are too predictable," he said.

"Less than dolphins," Kir said. "Less than any other organic being."

"Because we kill each other over ideas? Over nothing?"

"Because you can think your way beyond your nature."

"Robots do that," Laughton said.

"We have no nature," Kir said.

That fell on Laughton like a weight. All of his life robots had been people to him. That was perhaps the key difference between his thinking and Smythe's. It was about living with them and judging how they would react. Hell, Kir was his best friend. But he was, at base, a machine.

"I recorded the dolphins for Erica," Kir said. "I'll send it to you."

"Thank you," Laughton said, wanting to say more but not sure what that was.

Kir returned to the engine, and their speed picked up again. Laughton now scanned the horizon for the telltale appearance of more fins, but they didn't see any more.

———

That afternoon, Laughton and Kir were back in the same room they had stood in the day before, in front of the same panel of robots from all of the different branches of the robot government minus Sysigns. He remained decommissioned in some army stronghold.

"The antivirus patch works," Pattermann said to the room. "We expect all robot forces to be removed from the preserve by the end of the day."

"What about the fact that the virus originated from a human terrorist," Brandis said. "We're supposed to just leave ourselves open to further attack?"

"One extremist does not make the entire human population culpable," Pattermann said. "And the fact that a high-ranking robot in the military had access to the antivirus but had not released it doesn't sound too good."

Brandis's face remained impassive, but Laughton knew he must have been seething. At last, Brandis shook his head. "No. A single human extremist released the virus as a terrorist attack, and Chief Laughton here neutralized the hostile and delivered the antivirus as a good citizen."

"And who was this hostile?" the commissioner said.

"The hacker. What's his name? Who started it all."

"You want to claim someone killed days ago only just now produced the antivirus?" Kir said. "I'm sorry, the HHS isn't going to go along with this. It still makes this a human security breach. Popular sentiment for the preserve will still take a blow."

"And what do you think happens if popular sentiment turned on the military?" Brandis said. "You need us to be able to protect the preserve, don't you?"

There was a moment of silence while everyone made their own calculations. At last, Laughton said, "Why make it complicated? McCardy killed Smythe. We got McCardy. Simple."

"And the antivirus?"

"McCardy's a hero. Tried to stop Smythe and then turned out to have the antivirus."

Silence again.

The commissioner said, "I don't like it."

"It's the truth," Pattermann said.

"But not the whole truth," the commissioner said.

"Good enough."

The robots stood. Laughton wasn't sure what he felt about any of this. Was it really what was best for humans? Having the military owe them could be more valuable than anything. He rolled his shoulders, wincing at the bruise from where he had fallen back during his fight with Sysigns. He was just tired. So tired. He wanted to go to bed.

But the press conference came first. When the commissioner called him forth to receive a medal, he smiled, and said thank you, and left it at that. After the ceremony, he found his truck in the police department's lot. Kir walked him out.

"I've got to go back to Washington," Kir said.

"You going to come see Betty and Erica? Say goodbye. You need to show Erica the dolphins."

Kir shook his head. "I've got to make sure that everyone stays on script. I don't trust any of those bastards. I need to be on hand."

"The whole thing sucks," Laughton said. "Fucking make an orgo the sole bad guy."

"And an orgo the good guy," Kir said.

"Because that's what robots are going to hear," Laughton said, sarcastic.

"Listen. Come back to Washington with me. Now you're a hero. You'll have a lot of clout. You want to protect people? This will protect people."

"I wanted away from all of this. The preserve is supposed to be a safe haven."

"Then make it that for others."

"Betty would never leave. She's doing important work here. Work that can't be done anywhere else, that's much more essential than me being a politician. You've got that handled."

"You're exhausted," Kir said. "You look like hell. Rest, and think about it. It feels too good to have you by my side. I miss it."

Laughton sighed, and held out his hand. "Me too."

Kir took Laughton's hand and pulled him into a hug. The robot squeezed him tight, just short of hurting him. "Hero," Kir said, releasing him.

"Partner," Laughton said.

Kir opened the door to the truck, and Laughton climbed in. He pushed the on button, and once the GPS came online, he tapped "Home."

———

It was dark when Laughton arrived home, just past Erica's bedtime. The whole left side of his face tingled, like pins and needles, and it made his eyelids heavy. He had to imagine falling into bed in order to gather enough energy to leave the truck. He got out, then remembered the medal, and reached over the driver's seat to retrieve it from the passenger side. He wondered if they had a box of them at headquarters that they were able to produce one on such short notice. It had a Charleston Police Department seal on one side, an elongated octagon with a large double-masted clipper ship, which was the logo the city used before the creation of the preserve, so, yeah, they were probably working their way through back stock. They'd engraved the flat side with his name, the date, and the phrase "For service to robot and human safety." Had to get that "robot" in there.

The door to the house unlocked at his touch, and he let himself in. Betty was nestled in one corner of the couch, her feet curled up beneath her, her phone in hand held ten inches from her face. She dropped it into her lap to greet him. "Hey," she said.

"Hey."

"She wanted you to come in when you got home," Betty said. She held both arms out to him without getting up.

He crossed to the couch and collapsed next to her, leaning back so she could wrap her arms around his chest and hold him. All of his muscles relaxed, sinking into her. It made the fight he'd had on the boat feel impossible, unreal. How could he have almost lost all of this? He knew he should probably have felt angry, but all he felt was anxious, like a delayed reaction, all of the fear that he must have been carrying for the last few days flooding him now.

"Crisis averted," Betty said.

He held up the medal and she took it. She read it, and said, "What, do they just have these lying around?"

He grinned. "That's what *I* thought."

"I'm sorry," she said, dropping it on the couch next to them. "Congratulations."

"Thanks."

"And I'm sorry for freaking out on you."

"It's okay to be scared," Laughton said.

"Yeah, well . . ."

The indelicate *thump, thump* of feet coming down the stairs made Laughton roll his eyes, and Betty said, "Shit."

"Daddy, are you coming?" Erica said. She had come down just far enough that she could peek through the top of the banister to look at them.

"He's coming," Betty said. "Get back in bed."

"When is he coming?"

"Get back to bed," Betty said, exasperated. Guess he had missed a normal bedtime, i.e., frustration hour.

But this was the point, Erica was the point, the thing that made them human, that made the preserve imperative, that was both the recipient of his legacy and his legacy itself. "No," he said, raising his legs to use them as a counterweight, lifting him off the couch as he dropped them to stand. "I'm coming now."

"I told her you'd come in when you got home," Betty said.

"I'm coming," he said, halfway to the stairs.

"She was supposed to wait."

Erica was in her panda pajamas, her white torso floating over black legs halfway up the stairs.

"Go on," Laughton said. "Up."

Erica turned, and trotted back upstairs, running ahead of him. Her bed hit the wall with a crack as she leapt into it, laughing.

"Settle down," he said, coming into her darkened room.

She threw the covers off her face and yelled, "Boo," and then laughed and rolled back and forth on the bed.

"Erica." She kept laughing. "Erica. Erica, stop!" And she always made it so difficult. He knew that she was excited to see him, that she knew enough about what had been going on to have been scared as well, but knowing that was what was causing the behavior didn't make it easier to handle. The discomfort in his face tightened. "If you want me to tuck you in, then stop."

She settled, curling up, allowing him to cover her. "Will you sit with me in the dark for five minutes?"

Laughton sat down on the edge of her bed, and then leaned over her, kissing the top of her head, and then allowing the weight of his upper body to rest on her. She liked feeling the two of them squished together. He had to struggle to not fall asleep.

"Mom said everything's okay now. You fixed it," she said.

"And Uncle Kir," Laughton said. "And others. Not just me."

"But mostly you," she said.

The hero worship felt better than any medal, and Laughton smiled in the dark. They were both quiet for half a minute. Then it occurred to Laughton to make sure if Erica knew what had happened at all. "You know what happened?" he said.

"You found the antivirus that's going to stop robots from dying, so they're going to leave the preserve alone," she said.

Of course she knew exactly what was going on. She was Erica. "Yes," he said.

"Will they really leave the preserve alone?" she said.

"Yes," Laughton said. "For now." Betty would have been annoyed at him for adding the "for now," but he didn't believe in shielding Erica too much. Not knowing could be worse than knowing. "Probably for good," he said. "There are enough robots who support it. It's convenient to have us out of the way. If that's a good thing."

"Why wouldn't it be a good thing?" Erica said.

"I don't know," he said, not wanting to get into the thoughts he'd had on the boat, about the importance of learning how to live together and share. It made him remember the dolphins. "We saw dolphins today," he said.

"Eeeeee," she squealed.

"Uncle Kir videoed them. I'll have him send the video tomorrow." If he said he already had it, she'd want to watch it then, and that would only wind her up again.

"So jealous," she said.

"I said you'd be jealous."

"Can we go see them too?" she said.

"Maybe we can try," he said.

Erica was silent for a while then, but holding her breath, clearly thinking something more.

"What?" Laughton said.

"I don't want to leave the preserve," she said.

Hearing her say it, a part of him inside sank, and he realized that maybe he *had* wanted to go to Washington with Kir, join the Department of Health and Human Services, protect everyone, not just Liberty or even Charleston. But his mind settled back into the shape of their life here, in stark opposition to the assault on the island, and he knew, they wouldn't ever leave Liberty. "We're not going anywhere," he said. "You don't have to worry about that."

She was quiet for another half minute, and then said, "I love you," twisting under him to settle on her side.

He sat up, leaned over, and kissed the top of her head. "I love you, see you in the morning," he said. He pulled the door closed, but not latched, as he left the room.

The light was on in the bathroom, visible under the closed door. Betty was getting ready for bed. Laughton went into their bedroom to wait for his turn in the bathroom so he could brush his teeth, sat down on the bed, pulled off his shoes without untying them, and then lay back. The next thing he knew, Betty was tucking him in. He didn't wake up enough to go and actually brush his teeth, or even change out of his clothes.

"Good night," Betty said, close to his ear.

And with his last conscious thought, he hoped in the morning he'd feel recharged.

ABOUT THE AUTHOR

Ariel S. Winter was a finalist for the Los Angeles Times Book Prize, the Shamus Award, and the Macavity Award for his novel *The Twenty-Year Death*. He is also the author of the novel *Barren Cove*, the children's picture book *One of a Kind*, illustrated by David Hitch, and the blog *We Too Were Children, Mr. Barrie*. He lives in Baltimore.